LONG SHOT

Timothy Tocher

Meadowbrook Press
Distributed by Simon and Schuster
New York

Library of Congress Cataloging-in-Publication Data
Tocher, Timothy.
Long shot / Timothy Tocher.
p. cm.
Summary: When her father accepts a job as girls' basketball coach in another town, fifth-grader Laurie reluctantly leaves old friends and teammates and faces new challenges with a new basketball team at a new school.
Publisher's ISBN 0-88166-395-6
Simon and Schuster ordering number 0-689-84331-3
[1.Basketball--Fiction. 2. Moving, Household--Fiction. 3. Fathers and daughters--Fiction. 4. Single-parent families--Fiction. 5. Friendship--Fiction. 6. Schools--Fiction. 7. New York (State)--Fiction.] I. Title.

PZ7.T5637 Lo 2001
[Fic]--dc21 2001030379

Editorial Director: Christine Zuchora-Walske
Editor: Megan McGinnis
Proofreader: Angela Wiechmann
Production Manager: Paul Woods
Production Assistant: Danielle White
Cover Illustrator: Paul Casale

Published by: Meadowbrook Press
5451 Smetana Drive, Minnetonka, MN 55343

www.meadowbrookpress.com

BOOK TRADE DISTRIBUTION by Simon & Schuster, a division of Simon and Schuster, Inc., 1230 Avenue of the Americas, New York, NY 10020

05 04 03 02 01 12 11 10 9 8 7 6 5 4 3 2 1

Printed in the United States of America

Dedication

To Judy, who shot hoops with
me on our honeymoon.

Acknowledgments

Special thanks to my editor,
Megan McGinnis, for her sound advice.

Meadowbrook Press thanks Kali Kimbrell,
Malia Kimbrell, and Claire Theibert for their insight
and Eric Backstrom for his basketball expertise.

Contents

Chapter 1

Traveling

It was just another game of two-on-two, no different from the thousands Laurie Bird Preston had played before. She and her best friend, Christy, against their neighbors, Jack and Nancy, on the driveway in front of the house she shared with her dad.

Yet this game was special. It was the last game Laurie would play in her hometown of Bradley, New York. As soon as one team scored the eleventh and deciding basket, Laurie would climb into her dad's Jeep for a four-hour drive downstate to Compton. Without even consulting Laurie, her dad had taken the job as the girls' basketball coach at Compton Middle School. Coach Preston and Laurie would live with his mother in the house where he grew up.

Whenever the ball was knocked out of bounds, Laurie would sneak a look at her dad. Coach Preston had finished loading the Jeep and was leaning against a fender, watching the game. He looked calm, as if moving meant nothing to him, and it made Laurie mad.

Laurie was tall for a fifth grader and solidly built, with a small nose and large blue eyes. A few tears rolled down her freckled cheeks, but the way that Laurie was sweating, no one noticed them. Her bouncing brown pigtails gave her a cheerful appearance.

With the score tied at ten points, Christy whipped Laurie a pass and cut for the hoop. Laurie faked a dribble, then threw a blind bounce pass to the spot where she knew Christy would be. Christy's shot kissed the glass before it dropped through the net.

"Game!" Christy shouted. Laurie started to celebrate, then she remembered what the end of this game meant. Christy ran to the foul line and gave her friend a bear hug. Laurie squeezed back.

"Nobody knows my game like you do, Laurie," Christy said. "I can't believe you have to move, just when we would have been teammates."

Christy had played for the Bradley Buccaneers last year and had enjoyed a winning season. The one thing missing from the team had been a top ball handler like Laurie. Now that Laurie was in fifth grade and eligible to play, the girls had expected to finish first in their league. But then Laurie's dad had announced that they were moving.

Laurie was too choked up to say anything, so she just squeezed Christy harder. How could her father make her leave her best friend like this?

Jack and Nancy wished Laurie and her dad their best. Christy walked her to the Jeep, where Coach Preston stood waiting.

"Don't forget to write," Christy said.

Laurie nodded. "And I've got your e-mail address—in case I ever get a computer," she said, looking pointedly at her dad.

Coach Preston sighed. "Christmas is only a month away, Laurie. You never know."

As they drove away, Laurie stared out the windshield, spinning her basketball in her hands. Coach Preston hummed his favorite tune, "We Are the Champions."

"I can't believe you took this job without even letting me see the school," Laurie blurted. "Suppose I hate it?"

"Laurie, you're going to love my hometown. I went to Compton Middle School myself. You can bet your freckles they still remember me there."

Laurie rolled her eyes. Her dad was a great coach, but outside the gym he was clueless, especially when it came to how she felt about things. He still thought it was the greatest thing in the world that she had three freckles on each cheek. Sometimes he talked to her as if she were a two-year-old.

"Besides," Coach Preston went on, "this move makes a lot of sense economically. Grandma's been struggling to keep up her house with the money Grandpa left. We've been paying high rent in Bradley, with not much left over for extras or vacations. If we live together, we'll all have a lot more money to spend."

"So I'm losing my best friend for money," Laurie wailed. "Turn the Jeep around, Dad, and I'll never ask for anything again."

"It's not just money, Laurie," Coach Preston said softly "Grandma's been lonely living by herself. We're the only family she has. When this job was offered, I had to take it."

"But I like Bradley," Laurie protested. She couldn't stop herself. "I don't want to go to a school where I don't know anyone I miss Christy already."

"Give it a chance, honey," Coach Preston soothed. "Maybe once we get settled, Christy can come visit for the weekend."

"Dad, you know Christy starts basketball practice Monday. She won't have time for anything but hoops and school."

"You won't either, Laurie. Don't forget you'll be playing for Compton."

"I bet they'll stink," Laurie snapped.

"I don't know if the Cyclones will be good, but they've got two things going for them," Coach Preston said with a smile.

"What?" she asked suspiciously.

"A great coach and a great point guard."

Laurie sighed.

By dusk, they reached Compton. Coach Preston smiled broadly as he eased the Jeep through the familiar streets.

"Here's our turn, Laurie," he said, flipping on the blinker. "Remember how you loved playing in Grandma's yard when you were little?"

Before Laurie could answer, they pulled up in front of Grandma's house. The smile left Coach Preston's face. Tangled weeds and fallen leaves choked the neat little yard he and Laurie remembered. The paint on the house was peeling, and the wooden front steps were leaning dangerously.

Coach Preston whistled softly to himself. "I told you Grandma needed us."

Laurie glared back. "Yeah, but do we need Grandma?"

Training Table

Not trusting the front steps, Coach Preston led Laurie to the back of the house. When they reached the door, Grandma was there to greet them.

Grandma wore a clean apron over a flowered dress. Her hair was pulled back into a tight bun. Laurie knew Grandma loved knitting, cooking, and anything else grandmothers were supposed to enjoy. She was like a grandmother in a storybook. The problem was that she expected Laurie to be a storybook little girl.

"Hi, Grandma," Laurie called.

"Laurie? Is that you? When I saw you through the window, I thought your dad had brought a boy with him," Grandma replied. She looked pointedly at Laurie's sweatpants and sneakers.

Laurie looked down at her outfit and sighed. "It's me, Grandma."

Coach Preston hugged his mother. "Hi, Mom. Anything to eat?"

"Come sit in the kitchen, and I'll feed you both in no time," she answered.

That was another thing Laurie knew she wouldn't like about living in Grandma's house: Meals were a big production. At home Laurie and her dad had eaten easy-to-make meals like pizza or hero sandwiches in front of the TV. But at Grandma's, everyone ate nutritious, homemade meals at the dining room table.

Laurie had to admit, though, that the delicious smells filling the house made her stomach growl. She joined her dad at the table, her basketball pinned between her feet and the chair legs. Her mouth watered as Grandma set a whole turkey in front of them.

"I'll bet you two didn't have much of a Thanksgiving yesterday," Grandma said. "We'll feast tonight and live off the pickings for the weekend."

"It sure smells good, Mom. Right, Laurie?" Coach Preston said, as he reached for the carving knife.

Laurie had to agree. She ate almost as much turkey, gravy,

stuffing, and sweet potatoes as her dad did. But she had to quit after one slice of pumpkin pie. She was so tired, all she wanted to do was take a shower and go to bed. Instead, she was left to wash the dishes while her grandmother and her father went into the living room. Coach Preston wanted to make a list of the jobs that needed to be done to get the house back in shape.

When Laurie finally crawled into bed, she hugged her basketball, thinking of all the things she would miss by not going to school in Bradley. No more walking arm in arm with Christy, laughing at jokes that no one else thought were funny. No chance to wear the Buccaneer uniform and play at Christy's side on a winning team. No more relaxed feeling of being where she belonged, with people who knew and liked her.

At last Laurie drifted off to sleep.

The next morning was sunny and crisp. Coach Preston managed to get Grandma's old lawn mower started. He cut the grass, weeds, and leaves, and Laurie raked them into piles.

By noon, they were starving, and Grandma called them inside for a lunch of thick turkey sandwiches. Laurie was enjoying hers until Grandma spoke up.

"Why don't you drive us to the mall this afternoon, Jim?" she asked Coach Preston. "I'd love to buy Laurie something pretty to wear to school on Monday."

Laurie's mouth was full, but she stopped chewing. She was trying to think of a way to let down Grandma nicely when her dad came to her rescue.

"Thanks, Mom, but Laurie's got plenty of clothes," he said.

"Besides, kids aren't really into dressing pretty any more."

"I could see that when I first saw her from my window," Grandma snorted. "I just thought with a nice new outfit maybe Laurie could set a good example, her father being a coach and all."

Once she was able to swallow, Laurie answered, "Grandma, it's very nice of you, but I really don't need a new outfit. Besides, I thought I'd work on my game this afternoon. I see there's a court right across the street."

"Basketball! Is that all you ever think about? When I was in school, girls had other things on their minds."

"Look, Mom," Coach Preston jumped in, "why don't I take you to the mall? I'll buy some boards to repair the front steps while you shop. Laurie can stay home and practice. On Saturday afternoons, people should get to do what they want."

Grandma didn't look pleased with the situation, but Laurie was relieved to have escaped an afternoon of dress shopping.

Stats

Fifteen minutes later, Laurie was dribbling her basketball across the street. She passed a slide and swing set and started her warmup routine on the court. She shot lay-ups and then gradually worked her way farther from the basket. Before long, the only sounds she heard were the bouncing ball and the swish of the net as she buried shot after shot.

For the first time since she and her dad had pulled out of the driveway in Bradley, Laurie felt relaxed. She had lost her home, her school, and her friends, but she still had basketball. Her game had traveled with her. Laurie knew that if she was going to make a name for herself in Compton, it would be through basketball. It was her special talent.

When she finally missed a shot and had to run down the rebound, she noticed a boy sitting on a swing. He seemed to be watching her, but when she smiled, he put his head down and typed away at some sort of electronic gizmo in his lap.

"Oh, great," Laurie thought sarcastically. "This is a friendly town."

Next Laurie practiced free throws. If she put just the right spin on the ball, not only would she make the shot, but the ball would bounce back to her after it cleared the net.

After one of her rare misses, Laurie sneaked a peek at the boy on the swing. She figured he must be playing an electronic game while he spun around and around on the swing. The chain was wound as tightly as Grandma's bun.

Laurie decided to take a break and get a cold drink from Grandma's fridge. She was about to cross the street when she heard the boy call, "A little help?"

Laurie turned and looked at him. "Did you call me?"

"Can you come here for a second?" he asked.

Laurie shrugged, passed the ball through her legs, and dribbled toward the boy.

"What's up?" she asked.

Up close, she saw that it wasn't a game but a computer on the boy's lap. All that spinning he'd done had caused the swing seat to rise. Now the chains were pinning his arms, and his toes were barely touching the ground.

"This is kind of embarrassing," the boy said, looking at the ground. "I got tangled up in the swing and can't get out."

Laurie tried not to laugh. The boy wore thick glasses, the frames bent in places at strange angles. His jeans had ragged knees, and the toes of his sneakers were scuffed so badly, she could see his socks.

"What should I do?" she asked.

"First take my laptop so I won't drop it," he answered.

Laurie took the laptop and set it on a nearby picnic table.

"Now, if you push the swing clockwise," he instructed, "it'll untwist and I can get loose."

Laurie twirled the swing around and around, and the boy did indeed get loose, but not without falling headfirst onto the dusty ground. When he had brushed himself off, he stuck out a dirty hand.

"Thanks. I'm Howard, Howard Goldstein."

"Laurie Preston," said Laurie, extending her hand. "My dad and I just moved into that house across the street." She pointed at her grandma's house.

"Will you be going to Compton Middle School?" he asked.

Laurie nodded. "Grade five. How about you?"

"Grade five," Howard beamed. "Did you know that you made 94.3 percent of your foul shots just now?" he asked.

"You're kidding, right?"

"Hand me my laptop, and I'll show you."

To Laurie's amazement, Howard had charted her whole routine. He had recorded how many shots she had taken from each spot on the court and how many of them she had made.

"That's awesome!" Laurie said excitedly. "I didn't think you were paying attention. When I smiled, you didn't even say hello."

"Sorry. I get wrapped up in my numbers sometimes. Anyway, you're the best shooter I've ever seen."

"Thanks," said Laurie. She was about to invite Howard over to her grandma's house for a soda when he looked nervously over her shoulder.

"Uh-oh, gotta go. See you in school." Howard snapped his laptop shut and took off running. He tripped on the seesaw and sprawled in the dirt for a moment. Then he hopped up and rushed off again, brushing dirt from his laptop.

"Hey, How-weird, wait up!"

Laurie turned and saw two bigger boys. They began to chase Howard halfheartedly but gave up when he disappeared into a grove of trees. Laurie watched them turn back toward her. She scooped up her basketball and headed across the street. She might be new to Compton, but she sensed that these boys weren't worth getting to know.

On Sunday Laurie slept late. Then she enjoyed hot chocolate and cold cereal (her favorite breakfast) while she read the sports page in the *Compton Courier*. She wasn't impressed with the local paper. Its coverage of female athletes was limited to a one-column story on figure skating.

After eating a lunch of turkey hash, Laurie and her father went to work fixing the front steps. Laurie was the carpenter's assistant, which mostly meant she kept her dad company while he worked. But the job did give her a chance to complain without Grandma's hearing her.

"I know I'm stuck here," Laurie began, "but I'm not going to be Grandma's Barbie doll. If she bought me a dress yesterday, she can just take it back to the store."

"I talked to her," Coach Preston said, using a hammer to drive a nail deep into the wood with a single, well-placed blow. "Give Grandma a chance to get to know you. She hasn't been around a young girl in a long time."

"Doesn't she watch TV?" Laurie asked. "It's a new century, and she's telling me I look like a boy."

"Actually, she watches reruns of *Little House on the Prairie*," Coach Preston laughed. "I'll tell her to think of you as Laura Ingalls: You may be a tomboy, but you're still a fine young lady."

Laurie wasn't sure that advice was going to help her problem with Grandma.

Opening Tip

On Monday morning, Coach Preston drove himself and Laurie to school. Laurie hoped to ditch her father at the front door. She was afraid he would do something embarrassing, like give her a big hug in front of the other kids. But since she was a new student, they had to report to the office together and fill out paperwork. Laurie kept her head down as they walked through the hall, leafing through her binder as if looking for notes.

By the time she was registered, the school day had started. Coach Preston gave her a wink and a pat on the shoulder. He took her basketball and watched as she headed down the hall with Mr. Wright, the guidance counselor.

"See you at practice," he called.

Laurie dreaded walking into a classroom of strangers and being introduced. As she stood in front of the class, she wished she had her basketball to spin in her hands. Instead, she stared at the floor, bobbing her head once to acknowledge her new classmates.

The teacher, Mrs. Johnson, invited Laurie to take a seat in the back of the room. Three desks were empty, and Laurie was about to sit in the most isolated one when she spotted Howard.

It was so good to see a familiar face that she smiled broadly and scurried over to take the empty seat next to him.

A couple of the kids snickered and made kissing noises, which Mrs. Johnson shushed and Laurie pretended not to hear.

At noon Laurie and Howard walked to the lunchroom together.

"I was hoping you'd be in my homeroom," Howard said. "Sorry I had to leave so suddenly the other day."

"Who were those guys? Are they mad at you?"

"They're seventh graders, Butch and Eddie. They're not mad at me; they just like to torment me. I try to stay out of their path, but it's harder now that we're in the same school."

Having someone to talk to made lunch time pass quickly. But back in class, time stood still. Laurie checked the clock so often, she thought the hands were glued in place. When the bell finally rang, she hustled Howard out of the classroom. He wanted to walk her to the gym, but Laurie was so eager to play ball that he had to trot to keep up with her.

"Are you trying out for the boys' team?" Laurie called over her shoulder.

Howard was apologizing to a locker he had bumped into. He turned and answered, "Who, me? I'm a little clumsy, in case you haven't noticed. I'm going to offer to be the manager so I can go to all the games. Maybe Coach Adams will let me keep stats for him."

"Good luck," Laurie yelled as she sprinted down the hall to the gym. Her dad was waiting at the door with her gym bag. She grabbed it from his hand without breaking stride, like a relay runner taking the baton.

In two minutes she was dressed in shorts and a tank top and was shooting hoops. She glanced at the other girls trickling in and making their way to the locker room. Coach Preston rebounded for Laurie and fed her passes all around the key. Once Laurie found her rhythm, she went on a tear.

"Nice stroke, Laurie," Coach Preston called.

"Hey, Dawn, looks like you might have a little competition for high scorer this year," came a voice from the doorway.

Laurie felt good. Already the other girls were recognizing her talent. She turned to smile at the girl, but then she heard the girl's friend say, "She can't score without the ball, Jackie, and last time I looked, I was the point guard."

"Dawn, you've always got an answer," Jackie said, as she and Dawn high-fived each other and walked toward the locker room.

Chapter 2

Team Meeting

After he had the girls warm up, Coach Preston blew his whistle and had them sit in a circle. Laurie knew what would come next. For as long as she could remember, she had heard her dad give the same talk at each first practice of the year.

Sure enough, Coach Preston said, "How you practice is how you'll play." The familiar speech gave Laurie the opportunity to check out her new teammates.

When Coach Preston had been hired, the previous coach had called to tell him about the five returning players. From the notes her dad had taken and shared with her, Laurie could now pick the girls out. Opposite her were the two girls who had made the wisecracks about her shooting. Having heard their first names, Laurie figured they were eighth graders Dawn Adams and Jackie Morgan.

Laurie knew that Dawn was the daughter of the boys' coach and had been the star point guard of last year's team. Laurie now saw that Dawn was very pretty, with a blond ponytail and long, thin legs that were ideal for basketball.

Her freckle-faced friend, Jackie, played forward. Jackie had been the second high scorer on last year's team. Right now, while the other girls looked serious and eager to get off to a good start with the new coach, Jackie did not. Whenever Coach Preston turned his back, she would mouth his words and imitate his gestures. Dawn looked as if she would burst from suppressed giggles.

Next to Jackie was the biggest girl on the team, not in height but in bulk. Judging from the girl's size, Laurie knew she must be Jesse Jones, another forward. According to what Laurie's dad had learned about Jesse, she hadn't played much last season, but she had potential. Laurie thought Jesse looked nervous. Her dark skin glistened with perspiration as her eyes followed Coach Preston around the circle.

Jesse, too, took advantage of every time Coach Preston turned his back. She wasn't being silly, though. She was sneaking bites from a rather melted candy bar she had concealed underneath one of her wristbands.

The other two returning players were easy to recognize since they were identical twins. Marcie and Darcy Stone had been substitutes at both guard and forward. They had been described to Coach Preston as hustlers who looked to Dawn for leadership.

Laurie could hear the girl next to her breathing hard, even though they had been resting for at least five minutes. When Coach Preston asked the girl to introduce herself, she said, "Wheezy Lopez, seventh grade."

"What's Wheezy short for?" Coach Preston asked.

"She's short of breath, Coach!" Jackie interrupted.

Dawn and a few others snickered, but Coach Preston glared at them until they fell silent.

"It's all right, Coach," Wheezy said. "I've got asthma, so my breathing gets a little noisy sometimes. The kids call me Wheezy, but my real name's Luisa."

When Coach Preston turned to the girl next to Wheezy and asked her name, there was silence. She had long brown hair, which hid her face as she stared at the floor. She was obviously the tallest player trying out for the Cyclones, but she slouched as if trying to make herself invisible.

"And your name?" he tried again.

The girl's head snapped up, and she looked at Coach Preston in terror. Her eyes swept around the circle. When she saw the others looking at her, she covered her face with her hands and stared at the floor again.

Dawn and Jackie laughed hysterically. "That's Maggie or something like that, Coach," Jackie called between giggles. "She's from one of those weird countries in Europe and doesn't speak much English. I think she's kind of shy, too."

"Maggie, welcome to Compton and to our team," Coach Preston said gently to her bowed head.

Four more girls introduced themselves. Laurie knew it would take time just to learn everyone's name. How much longer would it take for them to become a team?

With his talk done at last, Coach Preston had the girls form lines for a lay-up drill. Laurie was on the rebounding side first. She had worked her way to the front of the line when Jesse shot an airball.

Laurie scrambled across the end line, caught up with the ball, and whipped one of her patented behind-the-back passes to the shooters' line. The next shooter was a slightly built girl with shiny black hair and eyes. She never saw the ball coming. Laurie's pass hit her in the chest and knocked her down. The other girls crowded around her, and Laurie hurried over to see if she was all right. Only Dawn and Jackie kept their distance, laughing as if they had never seen anything so funny.

Coach Preston helped the girl to her feet. To Laurie's relief, the girl seemed more embarrassed than hurt.

"I'm sorry—" Laurie began. She couldn't remember the girl's name.

"Li," the girl provided. "That's okay. I'll be ready next time."

Dawn spoke up, "Don't apologize to Little Miss Showboat, Li. Tell her to watch where she throws the ball."

"Yeah, that pass could have hit any one of us," Jackie added.

Laurie looked to her dad for support, but he just blew his whistle and restarted the drill.

The girls worked on chest passes next. Laurie was paired with a tall, thin girl named Angela Carillo. While Coach Preston was explaining what he wanted them to do, Angela jumped in place. Once the drill started, she bounced on her toes between passes.

"You put a nice spin on your passes," Angela called to Laurie.

"Thanks. My dad," Laurie said, pointing toward Coach Preston, "is big on that. He says when someone misses a pass, it's almost always the fault of the person who threw it."

"It must be cool to have a dad who's a coach. You must know everything about basketball!"

"I wish!" Laurie said. "Did you play last year?"

"No," Angela replied. "Chess is my game. But my folks have been bugging me to get more exercise. I figured I'd give basketball a try."

"Who do you play chess with?" Laurie asked. She and her dad liked to play, though neither one of them was especially good.

"Do you know a guy named Howard? Skinny, always carries a laptop?"

"He's one of the few people I do know at Compton," Laurie smiled.

"Most of the kids tease him, but he's really a nice guy when you get to know him," Angela said.

Laurie didn't know Howard that well, but she had decided that he was a nice guy the day he had recorded her stats on the playground.

Practice ended with three laps around the gym. Laurie ran her hardest and beat everyone but Li. Li had seemed lost during most of the drills, but there was no denying her speed. "She might not know much about basketball, but she sure can run," Laurie thought.

Coming in last were Dawn and Jackie, who had jogged along, talking and laughing, unconcerned with who passed them. They had run all the drills the same lazy way. Practice was over, and they had barely broken a sweat. Laurie smiled, thinking what tortures her dad would have in store for them in the weeks ahead. She knew her dad didn't care how good an athlete someone was as long as she tried her best, and Dawn and Jackie certainly weren't trying their best.

Garbage Time

Laurie grabbed her gym bag and walked to her dad's office. Coach Preston was sitting behind his desk, the phone book open in front of him.

"How soon are we leaving?" Laurie asked him.

"Is thirty minutes, okay? I need to make a few phone calls I didn't get to during the school day," he said. "You can start your homework if you want."

"I thought I'd go see how this guy Howard made out. He's with the boys' team on the other side of the gym."

Coach Preston grinned, "First day in school and a boyfriend already? Meet me back here in half an hour."

Laurie ignored her father's teasing and left.

Compton Middle School had a big gymnasium. When it was used for more than one activity, like it was today, the coaches slid a divider across the middle to create two smaller gyms. Laurie walked down the hall toward the entrance to the boys' side of the gym.

As she walked through the doorway, she noticed two holey sneakers sticking out of a wheeled Dumpster parked nearby.

"Howard, is that you?" Laurie asked.

"Hey, Laurie, grab my feet!" came Howard's muffled voice. Laurie pulled and Howard pushed with his hands until they managed to lift him over the edge. He collapsed on the floor at Laurie's feet, paper scraps and dust bunnies stuck in his hair. He reached inside his shirt and pulled out his laptop.

"Lucky I saw those guys coming!" he said. "I managed to tuck this baby in my shirt for safekeeping."

"Was it Butch and Eddie again?" Laurie asked.

"Yeah, they're on the basketball team, and this was their way of telling me they don't want me around. Too bad. I think I would have been a good manager."

"Why should you quit? Let's go see Coach Adams," Laurie suggested. "He'll tell those guys to leave you alone."

"I don't know," Howard frowned. "Butch and Eddie might be real mad if I show up at practice again."

"Do you want to spend the whole year running from them?" Laurie asked.

"I'd probably be in great shape by June," Howard joked. "But I would like to be manager, so let's try."

They walked to Coach Adams's office at the end of the gym and tapped on the open door. Dawn looked up in surprise from the math homework she was doing at her father's desk.

Coach Adams stared at Howard. "What's up, kid? You look like you mopped the floor with your hair."

Dawn chuckled and leaned back in her chair to listen. Howard brushed his hair absently and didn't speak until Laurie poked him in the ribs.

"A couple of the players don't want me as manager. They threw me in the Dumpster and told me not to come back."

Coach Adams laughed. "They're a feisty bunch this year. Should be great scrappers. Well, Howie, here's the story: If you want the job, stand up to those guys. Earn their respect. Otherwise, maybe you should quit."

Laurie couldn't believe her ears. Coach Adams hadn't even asked which boys had bullied Howard. She knew she should keep quiet, but she couldn't help herself.

"Coach Adams, don't you think the boys who did this should be punished?" she asked, her eyes flashing.

"Young lady, this is a guy thing. Boys have these little tussles.

If Howard wants to hang out with my team, he's got to take care of himself."

Coach Adams stood and started out of the office. "Come on, Dawn, I'm starving."

Gathering her books, Dawn smirked at Laurie. She inched past Howard as if he might contaminate her and followed her father across the gym.

"Maybe you'd be better off managing the girls' team," Coach Adams called over his shoulder. "I don't think Dawn would pick on you too much."

Dawn looked back, raising one eyebrow as if considering whether Howard was worth picking on.

"Do you believe that guy?" Laurie asked Howard when Coach Adams and Dawn had left the gym.

"He did have a good idea," Howard said, smiling at Laurie. "You could talk to your dad for me, and I could manage your team instead. Basketball is basketball. I don't care if girls or boys are playing as long as I'm close to the action."

"I guess he will need someone else now that I'm old enough to play. Until this year I always managed his teams. I'll ask him tonight," Laurie promised.

Laurie wasn't sure her dad would like having a boy for a manager. Howard wouldn't be able to run in and out of the girls' locker room the way a girl would. She decided to ask after supper, when her dad would be relaxed.

Free Agent

For supper the Thanksgiving turkey was back (in what Laurie hoped was its final appearance) in a steaming soup. Laurie tried to use her best table manners, but she found it hard to eat when her grandmother kept peppering her with questions.

"What did you learn in school today, Laurie?" she began.

Laurie had been so rattled about being in a new school that she had spent most of the day thinking of Christy and of her life in Bradley. The class might have been studying Chinese for all Laurie could remember.

"Oh, you know, the usual," Laurie answered.

"How could it be usual when it was your first day?" Grandma wondered. "Do they still teach home economics in the schools?"

Coach Preston laughed. "Those days are gone, Mom. They teach life skills to both boys and girls, but not in fifth grade."

"Well, I think it's high time they got back to teaching it. When I was Lauric's age, I knew how to sew and bake. I've used those skills all my life."

"But could you dribble behind your back?" Laurie couldn't resist asking.

"Don't be fresh, Laurie," Grandma snapped. "You spend too much time in gyms. That's why you dress and act like a boy. When you get older, how are you going to attract a boyfriend?"

"If I want a boyfriend," Laurie retorted, "I'll find one who thinks like I do: that girls can do anything boys can do."

Grandma opened her mouth to respond, but Coach Preston broke in.

"Laurie's got a boyfriend already, Mom. First day in the school, too," he teased. "What's his name again, honey?

"Howard is *not* my boyfriend, Dad. He's just a kid I know."

She had been about to ask if Howard could manage the team. But now she thought if she did, her father would be convinced Howard was her boyfriend. Maybe she'd wait until tomorrow morning to ask.

The doorbell rang just as Grandma was bringing a freshly baked apple pie to the table. When Laurie opened the door, there stood Howard, bits of garbage still in his hair, his laptop tucked under his arm.

"Hi, Laurie, I've got some stats I wanted to show your dad. I'm going to help him make this team something special!" Howard said enthusiastically.

"Laurie, who's your friend?" came Grandma's voice. "Ask him in for some pie."

"This must be Howard," said Coach Preston, who had followed Laurie to the door. He stuck out his hand.

Howard shook hands and said, "Coach, you won't be sorry you gave me the job. Take a look at some of the statistical breakdowns I can do for you."

Coach Preston looked at Laurie, hoping for some explanation of what Howard was talking about. But Howard didn't notice the coach's confusion. He strode into the kitchen and set his laptop on the table. Coach Preston followed and looked over Howard's shoulder.

"I can chart free throws and keep stats for each and every player," Howard explained. "That way you'll know who you'll want handling the ball at crunch time. I can't imagine anyone being a better shooter than Laurie, but the other teams will probably try not to foul her—"

"Uh, Dad," Laurie interrupted, "I was supposed to ask you if Howard could manage the team, but I never got around to it."

"Oh, a manager, sure," Coach Preston smiled. "The job is yours, son, but it involves filling water bottles and passing out towels. I'll take care of the coaching."

Howard looked as if he might protest, but Grandma had cut him a huge wedge of apple pie, and he was soon too busy eating to worry about statistics.

Eye in the Sky

The next morning, Laurie was walking up the front steps of the school when she heard Howard calling her name. She looked around, but he was nowhere in sight.

"Up here!" he called.

Laurie looked up and saw an arm waving from the top of the giant evergreen that grew next to the steps. She sighed and walked over to the tree. The ends of the lowest branches touched the ground, and Laurie parted two of them and walked inside. It was like being in a cool, green tent. The bright sunlight filtered through the needles. There was space for her to stand, yet she was hidden from anyone on the steps.

Howard's laptop leaned against the trunk. Laurie could see Howard climbing down, the branches so close together that even he would have trouble falling.

"Pretty neat, eh?" Howard said as he stepped down next to Laurie, his pants and shirt covered with blobs of sap. "It's my secret observation post here at school. I can climb up and check the whole neighborhood for Butch and Eddie."

"Maybe they'll leave you alone when they see you're not going to be the boys' manager."

"I hope so. But in the meantime, I'm trying to stay out of sight when there are no teachers around." Howard looked closely at Laurie. "You look tired. Didn't you sleep?"

"I was up until eleven finishing my homework," Laurie explained. "Then I had to write my best friend a letter. I started telling her everything that's happened since Friday, and before I knew it, it was one in the morning."

"Yuck, snail mail!" Howard made a gagging noise. "Why didn't you e-mail your friend? She'd have your message when she pops on her computer today."

"I know this may be hard for you to believe, Howard, but not everyone has a computer," Laurie said.

"Oh, the horror! I've heard of poor unfortunates like that. Why don't you use mine?"

"Cool! Can I send her an e-mail tonight?"

"Tonight and any night you want. How about right after supper?"

Just then the first bell rang. Howard peeked from between two branches. When he saw that no one was looking their way, he and Laurie stepped out into the sunshine.

Double Dribble

That afternoon, the Cyclones were back in the gym, ready to practice.

"We'll start with dribbling drills today, ladies," Coach Preston announced. "Dawn, Jackie, Li, and Laurie, you're up first."

The four girls lined up on the end line, each with a ball. Laurie wondered what her father was up to. She knew every drill he ran, and she hadn't seen this one before.

"It's simple," Coach Preston said. "When I say go, dribble as fast as you can to the opposite end of the court and back. Ready, go!"

Laurie tossed the ball out in front of her and raced after it. She loved speeding down the court, her head high, her hand effortlessly meeting the ball. At the far end, she put a dribble between her legs, spun around, and started back up court. She heard a few of the girls gasp.

"Eat your hearts out, girls!" she thought.

Laurie reached the end line first, with Li a couple of strides behind her. Dawn and Jackie loped in several seconds later and started to sit.

"Sorry, girls," Coach Preston called. "Thc two winners sit. You two go again."

Coach Preston already had two girls, Shirley Chase and Eileen Riley, both thin and athletic looking, poised on the line with basketballs. Before Dawn and Jackie could protest, he yelled, "Ready, go!"

This time Dawn and Jackie gave it all they had. But the

quick start had taken them by surprise. Against two rested dribblers, they finished third and fourth. Without allowing them a breather, Coach Preston sent them off again, this time against Darcy and Marcie.

Now Laurie understood what he was doing. Instead of yelling at Dawn and Jackie for goofing off, Coach Preston was showing them what would happen if they didn't give their best.

The twins were not very good dribblers. They had to watch the ball to keep it under control, which slowed them down. But Dawn and Jackie were on their third trip and were badly winded. They tried to pull ahead of the twins but still lost.

Angela and Maggie were next. Angela won easily, but Laurie had been sure that, despite how tired they were, Dawn and Jackie would beat Maggie. But Maggie's long, gangly stride—plus an accidental kick that had sent her ball halfway down the court, which Coach Preston had pretended not to see—allowed her to cross the end line just ahead of Dawn and Jackie.

Wheezy and Jesse were now the only pair left. And when they beat the exhausted Dawn and Jackie, they high-fived and hugged each other.

Dawn and Jackie were too tired to complain, but Laurie could read their anger in the glares they were sending her dad's way.

Before the two girls could catch their breaths, Coach Preston called for a scrimmage. He had Dawn and Jackie bring the ball up for one team, while Li and Laurie would handle the ball for the other.

As the teams lined up to start, he whispered to Laurie, "Push it!"

Laurie's eyes lit up. Her dad had just given her permission to play at full speed. She put her hand on Li's shoulder and said, "As soon as they shoot, break for the basket."

As Dawn brought the ball up court, Laurie hounded her, challenging every dribble. Jackie was taller than Li, which enabled her to take a pass from Dawn. Jackie faked Li, shot a jumper, and missed. Laurie was on the rebound in a flash and heaved the ball up court.

Li had broken for the basket the second Jackie had released her shot. She was waiting for Laurie's pass. It took Li two tries to make the lay-up, but because Jackie was slow getting to her, she had plenty of time to take the shots.

Jackie inbounded. Laurie tipped the ball away from Dawn, dribbled twice, and laid it in.

Li joined Laurie in pressuring the ball. She used her quickness to beat Jackie to spots on the floor, forcing Jackie to lose her dribble or throw the ball away.

Had Dawn and Jackie been rested, they could have made a respectable showing. But the combination of their rubber legs from the dribble drill and the pressure from Laurie and Li was too much.

Coach Preston let the scrimmage run for ten minutes before he called a break. Dawn and Jackie collapsed on the floor. Li hugged Laurie, and their teammates congratulated them.

Jesse and the twins, however, had walked away without a word. Laurie thought that maybe they didn't know whether to enjoy seeing Dawn and Jackie pay for their laziness or to worry that Coach Preston seemed to favor his new players over the veterans.

Laurie looked up at Howard sitting in the top row of the

bleachers, where he could see all the players and record their shots on his laptop. His head was down as he banged away furiously on the keyboard. She wondered if he had noticed how great she and Li had played together. Playing with Li had been almost as much fun as playing with Christy.

Coaches' Conference

After supper, Laurie got her dad's permission to go to Howard's house. She grabbed her basketball, flew out the door, and followed the directions Howard had given her.

When Laurie rang the doorbell, Howard opened the door with a warm smile.

"Hi, Laurie. Come on in," he said. "My laptop's up in my room recharging. I really should get a new battery, but I've been so wrapped up with practice, I haven't had time."

Howard began telling her about today's stats as he led her to his room. Laurie noticed that Howard's folks weren't home, and she wondered where they were.

Howard pushed open the door to his bedroom, which was anything but tidy. Glancing at an open closet door, Laurie couldn't help but notice several pairs of new-looking pants hanging inside. A stack of neatly folded shirts sat on a shelf. Two pairs of brand-new sneakers were on the floor.

"Howard, can I ask you a question?" Laurie said.

"Sure."

"If you have so many nice clothes, how come you don't wear them?"

"I'm not into style, Laurie," Howard shrugged. "My old things feel more comfortable, and I never have to worry if I spill something on them. It leaves me free to think about the important stuff, like chess, basketball, and computers."

The explanation made sense to Laurie. She felt most comfortable wearing sweatpants and a T-shirt. She would wear that outfit everyday, except she knew Grandma would never stand for it.

Howard showed Laurie how to use the e-mail program on his laptop. While Laurie typed her message, Howard whipped through his homework and ate a peanut-butter-and-jelly sandwich.

"If that's his idea of dinner," Laurie thought, "I can see why he got so excited about Grandma's apple pie."

She read over her message before sending it.

To: 2Christy@hitech.com
From: Howard1@hitech.com
Practice was great! Got to show the local girls a few of my smoother moves. Ate the lunch of last year's star player. Can't wait for practice tomorrow. Still miss you. My friend Howard is letting me use his computer. Write back at his address!
Long-Lost Laurie

When Laurie was ready to go home, she thanked Howard and left. As she walked home, Laurie dribbled her basketball with her left hand. Her dad had told her that her namesake, the great Larry Bird, used to do everything with his left hand for days at a time to strengthen it. By the time he got to the pros, he could pass, dribble, or shoot almost as well with his left hand as with his right.

When she arrived at Grandma's house, Laurie decided to check the fridge to see if there was any apple pie left. It would be a shame to let it get stale.

As she walked past the living room toward the kitchen, she heard Coach Preston talking on the phone. She stopped to listen.

"Coach Adams, how are you? Jim Preston calling." There was a pause, and then her father went on. "I'm planning a field trip for my team, and I was wondering if you would chaperone?"

He listened to the reply and then said, "Good. I thought I'd take the girls to Madison Square Garden on the twenty-sixth. Connecticut and Tennessee are playing in the Holiday Festival. You can? Great. If we're on the bus by noon, we'll be there for the pregame warmups."

Laurie couldn't believe her ears. Her father had been telling her about the famous New York City arena her whole life. Now she was finally going to see it. And two of the top college women's teams in the country would be playing besides.

"What's that, Coach?" Laurie heard her father ask. "I'm treating your daughter the same way I'd treat any player who slacks off. She's just been going through the motions. She needs to show some desire."

There was a long pause. Laurie wished she could hear what Coach Adams had to say.

"I'm sorry you feel that way, Coach. I might be new in Compton, but I've been coaching for ten years, and I think I know—Hello?"

Coach Preston slammed down the phone. Laurie decided to forget the apple pie. She slipped up the stairs to her room.

Chapter 3

Double Team

The next day at school, Laurie gave everyone she met a big smile. Maybe if she looked as if she were happy to be at Compton, people would be glad she was there. But only Wheezy, Angela, and Howard even bothered to say hello. Laurie tried not to be discouraged.

"When they find out what a great player I am, they'll all want to be my friends," she promised herself.

That afternoon, practice started with the usual meeting in a circle. Coach Preston gave a talk on hustle. Laurie guessed he was trying to warn Dawn and Jackie that he expected their best effort.

She looked to see if they were getting the message. To her surprise, the girls weren't sitting next to each other. Instead, Maggie sat between them in her familiar position, with her head down and her hair covering her face. Laurie couldn't even remember what Maggie looked like.

In yesterday's scrimmage, Maggie had slouched, doing her best to disappear in the pack of players. She hadn't looked to get open on offense, and on defense she had hung out under the basket. She'd tried to avoid contact, so shorter girls had pushed past her and stolen rebounds that should have been hers.

Today, when Coach Preston turned his back to the team, Laurie saw Dawn poke Maggie in the ribs. Maggie twitched and dropped her head even lower. Then Jackie poked her from the other side.

Maggie looked up. Her face was bright red, and she seemed about to cry. Laurie felt bad just looking at her.

Jackie called out, "Coach Preston, Maggie wants you."

He turned and saw the pain on Maggie's face. "Yes, Maggie?" he asked gently.

The added attention made Maggie look even more uncomfortable. She stared at the floor.

Laurie guessed her dad didn't want to press Maggie, because he went back to his talk about the importance of good defense. When he turned his back to the girls to demonstrate a proper stance, both Dawn and Jackie poked Maggie. She shook from side to side but didn't say anything.

Laurie couldn't believe the girls could be so mean. Maggie was too shy to complain to anyone. She'd never tell Coach Preston they were bothering her, and Laurie didn't want to tell on Dawn and Jackie.

At last it was time to run a drill. Coach Preston had the girls form two lines. Each player would sprint up court, get into a defensive crouch, and backpedal to the starting line.

Dawn and Jackie surprised Laurie by rushing to be first in each line. Maybe her dad was getting through to them. In her usual shy way, Maggie drifted to the end of Dawn's line. But with only twelve girls at practice, Maggie was soon up front. And since Dawn had run the drill first, she was now directly behind Maggie in line. Jackie was second in the other line.

Maggie teetered nervously, her right foot on the line. Coach Preston waved his arm to signal the start. At that instant, Dawn pulled back the waistband of Maggie's white shorts. Jackie dropped something down them. Maggie broke free and lumbered up court, veering from side to side and trying to reach down her shorts with one hand while she ran. Dawn and Jackie doubled over with laughter.

When Maggie reached the far end of the court, she yanked something from her shorts and threw it on the floor. She started to backpedal, but she stumbled and fell flat on her back, which made Dawn and Jackie laugh even harder.

Before Coach Preston could ask if she was okay, Maggie jumped up and finished the drill. But instead of going to the end of the line, she ran to the locker room.

Laurie ran up court and scooped up the object Maggie had pulled from her shorts. It was an ice pack. No wonder Maggie had been grabbing at it. Laurie backpedaled down court, flipped the ice pack to Howard, and trotted toward the locker room.

The locker room was dark. Laurie thought Maggie might have left the gym altogether, but then she heard a sob.

She walked into the bathroom and approached the corner stall. The sobbing stopped. Maggie must have heard her footsteps.

"Maggie," Laurie said softly, "come back upstairs with me. Dawn and Jackie were just trying to be funny."

Laurie didn't know how much English Maggie understood or could speak. She was about to speak again when she heard a husky voice from behind the closed door.

"They do not want me. Not on team, not in school, nowhere. At lunch they tease. Now at gym. I go away."

"Maggie, they're only two people. There are lots of other girls who want you on the team," Laurie insisted.

"I stink. I cannot shoot or dribble."

"You can learn, Maggie. With your height, you could be a great player someday."

"I want to be American, to play basketball. Why they won't let me?" Maggie asked.

Laurie squatted and talked to Maggie about being new and being lonely. She had come to comfort Maggie, but their talk was making Laurie feel better, too. Somehow it was easier to talk to a stall door than to another person face to face. She felt it was almost like talking to herself. At last Maggie opened the door. She smiled shyly at Laurie, then went to the sink and washed her face.

By the time Laurie and Maggie returned to practice, Coach Preston was ready to run a scrimmage. Dawn and Jackie were halfheartedly running laps, their punishment for disrupting practice. Coach Preston divided the other ten girls into two teams.

After ten minutes, he let Dawn and Jackie stop running, but he had them sit on the sidelines for the rest of practice. When practice was done, he called the two girls over. While the rest of the team raced to the locker room, Laurie hung back to hear what he'd say.

"Dawn, Jackie," he began, "if your attitudes don't improve, you're going to be watching instead of playing. It takes more than talent to win games. As veteran players, you should be helping build teamwork instead of tormenting your teammates."

"We were just having some fun, Coach," Jackie answered. "Newcomers expect to be tortured a little. It makes them appreciate being part of the team more when they are accepted."

"Yeah," added Dawn. "Jackie and I took plenty of guff from

the older kids when we first joined the team."

"I wasn't the coach then, but I am now. If you want to play for me, you'll treat everyone with respect," Coach Preston insisted. "Now hit the showers and come back tomorrow ready to help the team."

Jackie and Dawn headed for the locker room. As soon as they turned the corner, Laurie saw Jackie do her impression of the coach. Dawn's laughter carried back to Coach Preston, who shook his head sadly.

Freeze Out

"Ladies," Coach Preston began at the next day's practice, "our season starts January third, the first day of school after vacation. We host the Millbrook Tigers, Compton's oldest rivals. Way back when I was in school, the two games against Millbrook were considered the most important of the year. That means we're going to enjoy what's called a working holiday."

Several of the girls made faces, but Coach Preston went on.

"You're not in shape to play basketball. Five minutes of scrimmage and your tongues are hanging out. A team that's got some wind left in the fourth quarter can win a lot of games."

Coach Preston turned and made eye contact with each of his players.

"Here's the schedule for vacation: Be here at ten each morning. We'll work on conditioning from ten until noon. At one o'clock, we'll have our regular practice. If you miss a practice, you miss a game the first week we're back in school."

Laurie could see the girls exchanging glances. She wondered how many would make the commitment to get in shape.

Coach Preston had saved the good news for last. "December twenty-sixth we'll have our team holiday celebration. We're going to Madison Square Garden to see women's college basketball at its best: UConn against Tennessee."

The girls perked up at this announcement. Even Dawn and Jackie exchanged a high-five. Howard entered notes on his laptop. Laurie knew he'd later look up information on the two teams on the Internet.

Although high spirits carried the girls through their drills, trouble started when they split into teams for a scrimmage. Each day, Coach Preston had tried different combinations of players. Now for the first time, he put Dawn and Laurie on the same side. They were joined by Jackie, Jesse, and Angela.

Laurie was excited. She knew that if she was going to be a starter, she and Dawn would share the backcourt.

Dawn immediately took the point and brought the ball up court. Laurie worked to get free, but she was guarded by Li, who seemed to live to play defense.

Laurie couldn't shake Li, but since she was taller, she was often open. But Dawn never passed her the ball. Each time up court, Dawn either took a shot herself or passed the ball to Jackie. If Jackie couldn't shoot, she'd pass it back to Dawn. If Dawn was covered, Jesse or Angela might get the ball, but not Laurie. Laurie's only contribution to the offense was inbounding the ball.

After the scrimmage was over, the girls ended practice by running five laps. Laurie felt tears of anger well up in her eyes.

Why hadn't her father said anything to Dawn about passing to the open player? Her chance to play with the first string had come and gone, and she hadn't touched the ball. She ran as hard as she could, willing herself not to cry.

As usual, Li and Laurie were the first two to finish running. They made their way to the locker room and were half-dressed by the time Dawn and Jackie came in, followed by Darcy and Marcie. The four girls marched over to where Laurie sat lacing a sneaker. Li, who had been chattering happily, must have sensed something was wrong because she grew quiet.

"Look, fifth-grade hotshot," Dawn began, "I hope you got the message out there today. You can show off all you want in practice. But once the season starts, I'm playing the point. And if you want to see the ball, you'd better change your attitude."

Laurie didn't know what to say. "I'm just working hard to be a good player," she said weakly.

"You're daddy's little superstar," Jackie snapped. "You make the rest of us look bad with your showboating."

"If my father were coaching this team," Dawn said, "he'd sit you on the bench the first time you dribbled between your legs or threw a behind-the-back pass. What are you trying to prove?"

"And these losers," Jackie said, waving her arm to include Li as well as Maggie and Wheezy, who had just arrived, "are only pretending to like you because your father's the coach. They could never even make a real basketball team."

Laurie laced her sneaker as fast as she could and left without looking at Li, Maggie, or Wheezy. She was afraid they would look like losers to her, too.

She was quiet most of the way home. Her only words were "Dad, please!" when he started his third rendition of "We Are the Champions."

At dinner, Grandma was unable to get Laurie to respond to any of her questions. To break the silence, Coach Preston told his mother about the upcoming trip to Madison Square Garden.

"Jim, even during Christmas vacation you're going to have these girls thinking about basketball?" Grandma asked.

"Mom, except for Christmas Day and New Year's Day, most of their parents will be at work. They'll be glad the girls will have something to keep them busy. Practice will be good for them, and they'll have fun."

"Well, Laurie doesn't look very excited," Grandma pointed out.

Coach Preston took a closer look at Laurie. "Is something wrong, honey?" he asked.

"Just everything. You dragged me away from my friends, and then you made everybody in my new school hate me!" Laurie answered, more loudly than she had planned.

"Aw, come on, Laurie. You're making friends already. There's Howard. Li seems to like you. Maggie—"

"They're losers!" Laurie cut in. "They're only nice to me so they can be a part of the team. You taught me to play the game all wrong. The starters think I'm a showoff."

Laurie stood and stomped up the stairs. When she got to her room, she climbed into bed, clothes and all. When she reached for her basketball, she realized she had left it in the kitchen.

After a long, sad time, Laurie fell asleep. Soon after,

Grandma tiptoed into the room and gently placed Laurie's basketball in her arms.

Getting the Point

Laurie woke up early, hungry from missing supper the night before. She did her homework while she ate breakfast. Then, since there was still time before school began, she left her dad a note saying she was going to Howard's. She had to e-mail Christy.

She rushed over to Howard's house and followed him to his room. While Howard planned his next move in an on-line chess match with a boy from Montana, Laurie e-mailed Christy.

To: 2Christy@hitech.com
From: Howard1@hitech.com
Compton rots! The team stinks and the kids hate me. I miss you and the others.
Low-Down Laurie

Howard peered over Laurie's shoulder and read the message.

"Man, I knew you had a bad day yesterday, Laurie, but I didn't know you were that upset," Howard said.

Laurie told him what had happened in the locker room and at home with her father and grandmother.

"I thought I was the only one who had days like that," Howard responded. "Let's go downstairs. I haven't had breakfast."

Laurie sent the e-mail message, then followed Howard to the kitchen. It was weird: She had been to his house three times now, and she had never seen his parents. She did notice a vitamin pill and a note from Mrs. Goldstein on the kitchen table. Howard glanced at the note, pocketed the vitamin, and threw two frozen waffles into the toaster.

"My folks work a lot," he explained with a shrug when Laurie asked about his parents. "They come home late and go in early. I can page, fax, or e-mail them if I need anything."

Laurie didn't know who had it worse. There were times when it seemed as if her father was there every time she turned around. But she wouldn't want to be on her own as much as Howard was either. She wondered if Howard minded.

That afternoon, the team scrimmaged again, and again Laurie and Dawn were on the same side. Laurie waved her arms every time she was open, but Dawn ignored her.

Laurie did get her hands on the ball once. She stole one of Wheezy's passes, dribbled the length of the floor, and scored.

After the first break for substitutions, Coach Preston spoke to Dawn. "Switch spots with Laurie for a few minutes, Dawn. Let's try her on the point and you at shooting guard."

Dawn stared at Coach Preston, then reluctantly inbounded the ball. The change in the first unit was immediate. Laurie drove the lane and dished a perfect pass to Jesse, who laid it in.

Next possession, Laurie drew a defender away from Dawn, freeing her for an easy jumper. Dawn's soft shot barely moved the net as it dropped in for two points.

The Cyclones still had their share of missed passes and lost balls, but the team came to life with Laurie distributing the ball.

At the next break, an exhausted Li, who had spent the scrimmage chasing Laurie, put her arm on Laurie's shoulder and congratulated her. Dawn, Jackie, and the twins stood away from the others, talking softly.

As the team ran laps to end practice, Laurie wondered what Dawn and her friends had been talking about.

Final Cut

It was the last day of school before the holidays. The Cyclones sat in a circle while Coach Preston reminded them of the practice schedule during vacation.

Dawn raised her hand and announced, "Before I agree to spend my vacation in this gym, I want to know what position I'm playing this year."

"There are no set positions on my team," Coach Preston answered calmly. "I study what happens at each practice and in each game. I put players where I think they can best help the team."

"Well, this team did fine last year with me at point guard," Dawn said. "I earned that spot before you even got here. Either I play the point, or I don't play at all. And if I quit, my friends go with me."

Coach Preston looked Dawn in the eye. "If you're leaving, do it now so the rest of us can get started."

Dawn stood and walked toward the locker room. Jackie jumped to her feet and followed her. Marcie and Darcy looked at each other, then got up and left.

Just before she got to the doorway, Jackie called over her

shoulder, "Good luck against Millbrook. I hear they're loaded this year!"

Laurie saw that Jesse watched them go then turned her attention back to Coach Preston. Jesse obviously had chosen the new Cyclones—and the chance to play—over her teammates from last season.

Coach Preston looked at his eight remaining players. "Let's get started. Everyone's playing time just increased, so you girls have got to get in shape."

Laurie ran through the drills in a daze. She hadn't been happy that Dawn and Jackie had pestered everyone. But what kind of a team would the Cyclones be without them? It wouldn't be much fun playing on a team without experienced players. Jesse was the only one left from last year's squad, and as a fifth grader, she hadn't played very much. Shirley, Eileen, and Angela were in the sixth grade, but they hadn't been on the team last year.

Maggie and Wheezy were seventh graders but were new to the game. Wheezy's asthma had kept her from playing competitive sports. Maggie had only started playing basketball when she arrived in the United States a few months ago.

Li, like Laurie, was a fifth grader. What chance would the Cyclones have to win against teams made up mostly of seventh and eighth graders?

Laurie didn't blame her dad for standing up to Dawn. A coach had to make the decisions. He couldn't let any player tell him what to do. But she did blame him for bringing her to Compton in the first place. Laurie bet the Bradley team wasn't faced with any of these problems. Christy was one of a half-dozen girls who would be returning from last year's successful team, girls who were willing to do whatever was needed to win.

Laurie noticed that most of the Cyclones seemed to be as subdued as she was. Maggie looked frightened, and Laurie realized that the shy girl knew she was bound to play, now that there were so few girls on the team. All Maggie had probably wanted from being on the team was a quiet seat on the bench and the chance to make some friends.

While they shot free throws, Laurie's teammates spoke of their concerns. Wheezy said she worried that she'd have to play too many minutes, which would cause her asthma to flare up and lead her to make mistakes and lose games for the team.

Jesse admitted she was glad Laurie would be the point guard. She loved the soft passes Laurie threw as well as Laurie's knack for giving her the ball right when she needed it to score. But she also worried that she wasn't in good enough shape to play a lot of minutes. She pulled a soggy chocolate bar from under her wristband, jogged over to the sideline, and tossed it into a trash can.

Shirley said she had been thinking about quitting herself. She had a chance to visit her cousins in New York City over the vacation. There would be parties, skating at Rockefeller Center, and walks in Central Park. Now she felt she had to stay. She couldn't let the others down.

"All I wanted was some exercise," Angela said. "Now I've got to worry about making these shots. Coach will have to use me, whether he wants to or not."

"My dad will be happy," Eileen said. "He's convinced I can be a star if I get the chance to play."

"Are you that good?" Angela asked.

"Not even close, but he thinks that I just need to develop my talents. I guess we'll find out who's right this season," Eileen said, as Angela's pass bounced off her fingertips.

Only Li seemed thrilled with the new team. She jumped around as if she couldn't contain her excitement. She said that more than anything she wanted a chance to play, and it seemed that her time had come. She had made up her mind to run faster and work harder than anyone on the team.

Laurie looked up at Howard sitting in the top row of the bleachers. He must have been seeing the missed shots. He probably didn't need to look at his stats to know this was the worst shooting the Cyclones had ever done.

Laurie glanced at her dad sitting on the bleachers and staring at nothing in particular. She guessed he was too busy trying to figure how the Cyclones could make it through the season with just eight players to even notice their terrible shooting.

Two-a-Days

The weather was brisk but pleasant for December, so Coach Preston took practice outdoors. Laurie hadn't been looking forward to the extra practices. But now that Dawn and Jackie weren't there to cause problems, she found herself enjoying them.

The girls followed Coach Preston in long jogs around Compton, dribbling as they ran. The first day they had lost one basketball, which had bounced off Maggie's foot and been flattened by a passing pickup truck. But since that mishap, everyone's ball handling had been improving rapidly. Soon the girls had arrived at practice dribbling and left practice dribbling. Coach Preston had told them it would be a noisy Christmas Eve in the eight households where his players lived.

On Christmas morning the Preston family gathered around the tree in the living room. Laurie and her dad had gotten Grandma a sewing machine, which Coach Preston had seen her admiring at the mall.

Laurie gave her father a portrait of Larry Bird, his all-time favorite player, which she had painted in art class.

Laurie didn't know what gift to expect from Grandma. She was afraid Grandma might have bought her a dress or an apron, so she was relieved to see that the package was small. When she tore it open, she found a WNBA basketball game on CD-ROM.

"Thanks, Grandma," she said happily. "I can use it on Howard's computer. He said I could—"

"I don't know, Laurie," her dad interrupted. "The sun sets early now. I don't want you out after dark walking to Howard's house."

Laurie was confused. Why would Grandma give her a gift that her father didn't want her to use?

Just then the doorbell rang. Laurie noticed her dad and grandmother exchange sneaky smiles as she went to open the door.

On her doorstep stood Howard, carrying a tool kit under one arm and his laptop under the other. "Merry Christmas, Laurie," he said.

"Thanks, Howard. Don't tell me your folks are at work today."

"No, the stock market is closed. We're going out for breakfast in a little while. But first I have a job to do for your dad," Howard said, peering around Laurie at Grandma and Coach Preston, who now stood behind her.

"What job?" Laurie asked, but no one answered.

Grandma, still wearing her smile, led Howard upstairs. Coach Preston waved to Laurie to follow them, and he brought up thc rcar.

At the top of the stairs, they filed down the hall to a small storage room. "What job could Howard have in there?" Laurie wondered.

Everyone stopped at the door. "Open it, Laurie," her father said.

Laurie pushed open the door. There was a pile of boxes in the room, each topped with a red bow. As Laurie read the words monitor, tower, speaker, and printer on the labels, her face broke into a grin. She had her computer.

Laurie wrapped one arm around her father and the other around her grandmother and pulled them close.

Howard was in his element. A job that might have taken Laurie and Coach Preston all day he did in minutes. Before Laurie knew it, the computer was installed and she was sitting at the keyboard.

There was one final surprise. Howard reached in his jacket pocket and pulled out a cable. He inserted one end into the computer and plugged the other into a telephone jack.

"Now you can e-mail Christy whenever you want, Laurie. You're on-line."

Coach Preston and Grandma left Laurie to enjoy her present. She listened as Howard explained the computer's basic functions. She was installing her WNBA game when the doorbell rang.

"That will be my folks," Howard said. "Come on down and meet them."

By the time Laurie and Howard got downstairs, Grandma had the Goldsteins seated at the kitchen table.

Mr. Goldstein looked like a bigger, older version of Howard. He wore a necktie and white shirt, but the tie was stained, and his glasses were smeared with fingerprints. He also shared Howard's warm smile and friendly manner.

"It's a pleasure to meet you, Laurie," he said.

Mrs. Goldstein was equally friendly. "Howard has told us so much about you. I'd love to see you play sometime," she greeted Laurie.

Grandma said, "From what Laurie tells me, you two are at work all the time, so I doubt you'll be going to any games."

Laurie's face turned red. How could Grandma be so rude? She vowed never to tell her grandmother anything again.

But Mrs. Goldstein just laughed. "Frank and I do work a lot of hours. I used to stay home and try to take care of Howard." She mussed his hair affectionately. "But Howard's got his own mind. He eats and dresses the same way now as he did when I was fussing over him all day. Now I don't get so frustrated over it."

"I'm afraid he takes after me," Mr. Goldstein added. "The Goldstein men are too busy to worry about being neat."

Coach Preston tactfully turned the conversation to the middle school, and a few minutes later the Goldsteins left, with

Howard promising to come back and try out the WNBA game at his first opportunity.

Short-Handed

Not too many things could have lured Laurie away from her computer on the day after Christmas. But the chance to see two top women's college basketball teams play in Madison Square Garden was one of them.

She and her father had been up early that morning and were now out for a jog. Laurie let her dad set the pace, and she dribbled as she ran. Every once in a while, her father would wheel around and try to take the ball from her. Laurie was working on a move in which she dribbled behind her back on an attempted steal and drove with her left hand.

They were having a great time, enjoying the cold, clear morning and each other's company. When Coach Preston suddenly skidded to a stop in front of her, Laurie thought it was another ball-stealing ploy.

"We've got to get home!" he called and began running at full speed.

Laurie couldn't keep up with him until she stopped dribbling and tucked her basketball under an arm. Even then, she was badly winded by the time they reached Grandma's house.

"Dad, what's the matter?" she gasped.

Coach Preston was panting, too, as he raced up the steps and into the house. He pulled a list of teachers' names from a drawer in a table by the telephone.

"It just dawned on me, Laurie," he told her. "I don't have a chaperone for the trip. Coach Adams was supposed to go, but he canceled after Dawn quit the team."

An hour later, and only a half-hour before the bus was scheduled to leave, the problem still hadn't been solved. None of the few colleagues Coach Preston had been able to contact was available. The players' parents couldn't go either. And Howard had reported that his mom and dad were at work.

Laurie and Coach Preston were about to give up hope when they heard Grandma singing to herself in the kitchen. They looked at each other. Simultaneously they said, "Grandma!"

Considering that Grandma had no interest in basketball and wouldn't know Madison Square Garden from the Garden of Eden, she gave in to them pretty easily. Coach Preston had promised to paint the house as soon as spring came. Laurie had agreed to let Grandma buy her a couple of dresses for special occasions. And, of course, Grandma was allowed to bring her knitting.

The crisis averted, the minibus pulled away from Compton Middle School at five minutes past noon. The eight Cyclone players, Howard, Coach Preston, and Grandma were all on board.

Laurie had expected Grandma to sit in the front with her son. Instead, Grandma headed toward the back of the bus. She slid in next to Maggie, who was sitting alone, staring out the window.

"You should have a peaceful ride, Grandma," Laurie thought.

Howard had saved a seat for Laurie, and they passed the time pleasantly, playing games on his laptop.

The day after Christmas proved to be a great time for a bus ride from Compton to New York City. The Cyclones cruised down the lightly traveled highways. Without the swarm of commuter traffic, they passed through the Lincoln Tunnel without delay. In less than an hour, the driver dropped them off at the Thirty-Third Street entrance to Madison Square Garden.

Garden Party

The Garden was everything Coach Preston had described and more. Laurie didn't know where to look first. She scoped out the scoreboards with the names and numbers of the Connecticut and Tennessee players. She let her eyes roam through the stands, especially the front rows, where she had often seen celebrities sitting when she watched games from the Garden on TV.

Howard pointed to the jerseys hanging from the rafters in honor of players like Bill Bradley and Willis Reed, whose numbers had been retired forever. Laurie wondered when the first woman's jersey would hang in this famous arena.

Coach Preston told everyone how his father used to bring him to the Garden when he was a boy. As they walked to their seats, he acted out Rick Barry's underhand free throw, Kareem Abdul-Jabbar's sky hook, and other moves of the great NBA players he remembered.

Then he told them how he had played in the Garden during his senior year at Manhattan College. His team had lost the opening game of the National Invitational Tournament, but it had been a thrill to play in front of friends, relatives, and thousands of fans in this basketball shrine.

Grandma seemed unimpressed by her surroundings. She

brushed off her chair with her scarf before she sat, then concentrated on her knitting. Laurie saw her whisper to Maggie, who sat next to her.

Judging by the banners, sweatshirts, and cheers, most of the crowd was rooting for the University of Connecticut. Both schools had recently won national championships, but many UConn students and alumni lived in the New York area.

The Cyclones were divided in their sympathies. Some planned to cheer for the underdog, the Tennessee Lady Volunteers. Others decided to root for the Huskies, since they were a more local team and were the defending champs.

After the teams finished their warmups, the lights were dimmed and the starting lineups were introduced. As each player's name was called, she ran out onto the Garden floor, a spotlight shining on her and the crowd cheering. Laurie couldn't imagine how good it must feel to have strangers rooting for you.

Maggie and Grandma stood and clapped politely with the others. Then Dragana Coriz, a Tennessee guard, was introduced. Maggie began waving her arms and yelling at the top of her lungs. Laurie and Coach Preston looked at each other in wide-eyed amazement.

"She from Croatia, like me!" Maggie shrieked.

"Go, Tennessee!" Grandma hollered. One by one all the Cyclones started cheering for the Volunteers.

The game was a thriller. Neither team could shake the other, and there were few lulls in the action. Laurie noticed that Grandma had set her knitting aside at the opening tip and didn't pick it up again until halftime.

When Dragana Coriz hit a three-pointer to win the game in the final seconds, Maggie and Grandma danced in the aisle.

Coach Preston hugged Laurie and whispered in her ear, “It looks as if there’s one more basketball fan in the family!”

The happy mood followed them onto the bus. For the return trip, everyone took turns leading the others in a sing-along. Maggie and Grandma stood together and sang “God Bless America.” Coach Preston waited until last to sing “We Are the Champions.”

Laurie noticed that Jesse sat across the aisle from Grandma and Maggie. Between songs the three of them were having an animated conversation. It seemed as if everyone except Laurie was finding Grandma easy to talk to.

Chapter 4

Final Prep

The rest of the vacation passed quickly. All eight Cyclones, plus Howard, showed up each day for conditioning drills and practice. Since the team was short-handed without the four girls who had quit, Howard and Coach Preston filled out the sides for the scrimmages. Howard might have been clumsy, but he had a good understanding of the game. He knew where he belonged on the court and where to pass the ball.

Besides having fun at practice, Laurie enjoyed her free time. She found herself spending most of it with Li. Li was determined to become a good player and was eager to learn from Laurie. And beyond that, the girls found it easy to talk to each other. Laurie was beginning to feel as comfortable with Li as she had with Christy.

But one thing still bothered Laurie: Grandma. It seemed to Laurie as if Grandma watched every move she made and pounced on the chance to correct her.

"Sit like a lady, dear," she would say when she saw Laurie slouched on the couch, watching TV. Laurie couldn't understand why the other kids seemed to like Grandma so much better than she did.

Since the field trip to Madison Square Garden, Jesse and Maggie had begun stopping by the house. One afternoon when Laurie came home from shopping with Li, Jesse was there, dropping off some muffins she had baked using one of Grandma's recipes. Another day Laurie found her grandmother giving Maggie a knitting lesson.

When Laurie saw Maggie later at practice, she asked her about her relationship with Grandma.

"What did you and my grandmother talk about all the way to New York City and back?" Laurie began.

Maggie smiled. "She ask me about Croatia. I tell her about my grandmother and how I miss her."

"Did she try to boss you around?" Laurie asked.

"A little. She tell me to stand tall, be proud. That's what grandmas are supposed to do," Maggie said.

Laurie thought about what Maggie had said as she walked home with Howard. She asked for his opinion on Grandma.

"Your grandmother is a cool lady," Howard answered.

"That's easy for you to say," Laurie countered. "She doesn't try to dress you like a Barbie doll."

Howard was quiet for a moment. Then he said, "I don't see her doing that to you either. When was the last time she bugged you about your clothes?"

Laurie started to snap an answer, then realized that she couldn't remember exactly when the last time was.

"She still thinks about it. I can tell by the way she looks at me," Laurie mustered. "Besides, she was kind of rude to your parents, asking them why they work so much."

"My folks didn't care. They know not everyone has the same approach to parenting that they do. This works for us, so why worry if someone else doesn't like it?"

Laurie got even less support from Li when she called her that night. "My family is Chinese," Li said. "We believe that the older a person is, the wiser he or she becomes. Think of all the years your grandmother has experienced. Why shouldn't she give advice?"

Laurie began to think that maybe the problem wasn't just Grandma. Maybe she was to blame for their strained relationship, too.

Although she often thought about her relationship with Grandma, most of Laurie's time and energy went into thinking about the Cyclones. The starting lineup was set, and the girls seemed excited and confident. Laurie would, of course, be the point guard. Wheezy would join her in the backcourt. Wheezy was a solid player but not a good shooter. When she needed a breather, Li would bring her fresh legs, desire, and infectious attitude onto the court.

The forwards, Jesse and Angela, were two of the most improved Cyclones. Jesse was starting to realize her big body could be an asset. Jesse told Laurie that all her life, kids had teased her about her size and her huge appetite. They didn't realize that a big body needs a lot of fuel. In the past, she had eaten whatever she could get hold of, which was usually junk food. Now playing ball and cutting down on sweet snacks was paying off. Her extra flesh was turning into muscle. She might not beat the smaller girls to a loose ball, but if she was in position under the hoop, no one could move her. Once she got her powerful hands on the ball, it would be hers.

Angela was quick, but she still lacked strength. Dawn and Jackie had dubbed her "Angel Hair" because she was as thin and frail as angel hair pasta. She scrambled all over the court and was so active that she needed frequent rests.

The center position was the team's biggest concern. Maggie was developing a nice touch on shots under the basket and was, by several inches, the tallest player on the team. She was still shy, but at least now she talked to Coach Preston and her teammates without looking at the floor. On the downside, though, Maggie shunned contact. During scrimmages, if she and another player were after a loose ball, she would back off. And during games, the opponents would be a lot rougher on her than her teammates were during scrimmages.

Other than Li, there were only two players on the bench, Shirley and Eileen. Shirley played guard and forward and always gave a great effort. Shirley had told Laurie she was glad that she had given up her vacation in New York City to play ball. She was enjoying being part of a group.

Eileen was the backup in the middle. She was tall enough to be a center, but barely left the floor when she jumped. She worked hard to get good position under the basket. Laurie knew Eileen had only average ability but would never disappoint her father or Coach Preston by not hustling.

The Cyclones practiced on New Year's Eve day and then were off for the long holiday weekend. Laurie couldn't work on her game, as real winter weather had set in. A long-overdue snowfall covered the outdoor court. So she spent most of her free time on her new computer.

The night before the first game, she e-mailed Christy.

To: 2Christy@hitech.com
From: LBP@hitech.com
Happy New Year! Let's hope this is the year of the Buccaneers and Cyclones. Good luck this week.
On-line Laurie

She was about to log off when Grandma tapped on the door.

"Hi, Grandma, what's up?" Laurie asked.

Grandma looked embarrassed.

"Is it hard to learn?" she asked.

"Hard to learn what?"

"The computer. Do old people like me ever get as good as you kids?" Grandma wondered.

"It's not hard at all,' Grandma. What would you like to know?"

"My best friend, May Hopkins, moved to Florida to live with her daughter. She says they've got a computer. I was wondering if I could learn to send e-mail. We talk on the phone, but it's so expensive."

"Grandma, e-mail is a snap." Laurie slid to one end of the bench in front of the computer. "Sit down, and I'll show you how it works."

As she explained the process, Laurie realized that this was the first time she'd ever felt comfortable with Grandma.

Game Day

The next day, Laurie thought she might burst with excitement before game time. She had counted on Howard to distract her. But during lunch, he was so busy furiously typing on his laptop that they barely talked.

"What are you doing to that thing?" Laurie asked.

Howard covered the screen with his hands. "You'll find out this afternoon," he said. "I have to work quickly because the battery will die soon. It hasn't been fully charging lately."

He hunched over the keyboard and didn't lift his eyes from the screen until lunch time was over.

The second that school ended, Laurie hustled down the hall and into the locker room. She pulled on her uniform and admired the big blue "1" in the middle of her chest. She turned around, looked over her shoulder at a mirror, and smiled at the reflection of a cartoon cyclone printed on the back of her jersey.

Laurie stretched and then nervously dribbled her ball while she waited for her teammates to dress. Her mind whizzed as she imagined the upcoming game. She tried to picture the kids filling the bleachers. The boys' team was playing a road game, and not many students traveled to see them compete. So there should be a good-size crowd to see the girls' team play.

At last Coach Preston knocked and entered the locker room. "Ladies, we've worked hard for over a month. You're in the best shape of your lives. Let's go out and have some fun today."

With a whoop, the Compton Cyclones rushed out of the

locker room and up the stairs to the gym. When they started their lay-up drill, Laurie couldn't help but notice that the stands on the home team side were nearly empty. The first two rows behind the Compton bench held all their fans: one or both parents of each of the players and Grandma.

The visitors' side of the gym, on the other hand, was filling rapidly. Millbrook was only eight miles from Compton, and the Tiger fans were treating this like a home game.

During the shoot-around, Laurie went under the hoop, where Howard was rebounding and feeding balls to the Cyclones.

"Where is everybody?" she asked him. "What is there to do today that would keep kids out of the gym?"

Just then they heard a cheer from the other side of the gym. She looked at the divider questioningly.

"Volleyball," Howard explained. "Dawn and the others are on the volleyball squad. They've got a match today, too, and most of the kids are over there."

"But volleyball's an intramural sport. We're playing a real game against Compton's biggest rival."

"I know, but Dawn and Jackie have convinced everyone that only the losers are out for basketball. The cool kids are playing volleyball, so that's where their friends are."

"Fans or no fans, we're going to play good basketball," Laurie promised.

Howard pushed back his glasses and said, "And I've got a few surprises for the game, too."

The buzzer sounded, and the teams went to their respective benches. Howard got a good laugh from the crowd as he tried to gather the basketballs. Each time he grabbed one ball, he seemed to drop two more. Li and Laurie finally helped him round up the balls.

The crowd stood for the Pledge of Allegiance. Laurie noticed that Maggie knew every word. She said the Pledge as if she really meant it, her usually soft voice strong and clear. Laurie had often daydreamed when reciting the Pledge, but seeing Maggie proudly say the words reminded Laurie how lucky she was to live in the United States. She straightened her shoulders and raised her voice to match Maggie's.

Coach Preston called the girls for a final huddle. "Play hard and have fun," he said.

Laurie planned to do both.

Season Opener

Howard unveiled his surprise as the teams lined up for the opening tip. As she got herself into position on the floor, she glanced at Howard sitting alone in the top row of the bleachers, his laptop plugged into an outlet and connected to a boom box speaker. She watched him pound some keys, and suddenly peals of thunder and roaring winds echoed throughout the gym. The second it ended, he hollered, "Howl, Cyclones, howl!"

Howard waved his arms for the fans to join him. The few Compton fans glared at him, several with their hands clapped over their ears. Grandma had been so startled by the noise that she dropped her knitting needles. She later made Howard crawl under the bleachers to find them.

Laurie looked around the circle in alarm. Only Maggie was as tall as the Tiger player opposite her, and Maggie looked terrified. The roar from the Tiger fans (which now replaced Howard's sound effects) seemed to have put her in a trancc. She was staring straight ahead, her eyes blank.

The referee tossed the ball, but Maggie didn't jump. The Tiger center batted it to a teammate, who blew past Jesse and scored easily.

Wheezy inbounded and Laurie brought the ball up court. She planned to help her teammates relax by setting them up for some easy shots. But where were those teammates?

Laurie had expected Maggie to be petrified, but the other girls seemed to be, too. They stood paralyzed, making it easy for the defense to keep the Cyclones from getting the ball.

Laurie faked her defender and drove the lane. She might have scored, but at the last second, a Tiger player left Jesse and jumped in front of her. Instinctively, Laurie passed the ball behind her back and into Jesse's hands.

Jesse was taken by surprise, and the pass bounced off her hands and out of bounds. She had been ready to rebound shots if Laurie missed, not to take passes from her.

That play seemed to set the tone for the half. No matter what play Laurie ran, the Cyclones couldn't score. Those who did manage to catch a pass threw the ball back to Laurie as if it were a hot potato.

The Cyclones settled down when they were on defense, but they trailed 10 to 0 at the quarter and 18 to 4 at the half. Laurie had scored their only two baskets on steals.

Coach Preston reassured the team at halftime. "It's the first game of the year, and we were a little nervous. We'll do better this half."

Then he turned to Laurie. "Look for your shot more, Laurie. Maybe if you sink a few, the defense will loosen up on the other girls."

Laurie knew that the problem wasn't tight defense but tight Cyclones. No one else wanted the ball and the responsibility it carried. She thought that her dad probably knew that, too, but didn't want to make the others more nervous by pointing it out.

The Cyclones reluctantly went out to warm up for the second half. When they reached the court, Howard started the storm sound effects again. The Compton fans hooted him down, which made the Tiger fans laugh.

Laurie took her dad's advice in the second half. She looked for her shot and fired it up at every opportunity. Unfortunately, the Tigers soon figured out that she was the only threat Compton had. They double-teamed Laurie constantly. The shots she took were difficult, and she missed far more than she made.

During the fourth quarter, Mr. Riley, Eileen's father, began screaming that Laurie was a ball hog. Laurie wondered why he couldn't see that no one else wanted the ball.

Then, with about three minutes left, while a Tiger player shot foul shots, Laurie looked around the gym. At the far end, she spotted Dawn and a group of her friends. They must have wandered in after their volleyball match.

Laurie checked the score: Visitors 38, Home 14. They were getting slaughtered. She saw Jackie point at the scoreboard and say something. The whole group laughed.

Furious, Laurie rebounded a missed foul shot, put her head down, and raced up court. When a Tiger defender cut in front of her, Laurie slammed on the brakes and went up for a jumper. To her surprise, she was way behind the three-point line. Her shot barely grazed the rim.

Mr. Riley bellowed, "Pass the ball, gunner!"

Laurie felt her face turn bright red. She pictured Dawn and Jackie laughing hysterically. In seconds, she heard the chant, "Gunner! Gunner! Gunner!" which she was sure they had started.

The last two minutes dragged by. Both teams were tired, and it seemed that the only thing they had energy to do was to foul each other. By the time the final score of 41 to 16 was posted, even the players' parents had stopped paying attention.

Recognition

Over dinner, Coach Preston tried to lift Laurie's spirits. "Hey, kid, you did great for your first game."

Laurie managed a smile. Then he added, "Once you've played a little more, you'll have a better feel for when to shoot and when to pass."

The blood rushed to Laurie's cheeks. "Dad, I shot because I had to! No one else would. If I didn't shoot, we passed the ball around until we lost it."

"Some of the girls are shy, Laurie. But, really, a few times you were way behind the three-point line when you let it sail," Coach Preston went on.

Laurie's eyes filled with tears. Not only did the stupid fans think she was a gunner, but her own father did, too. Before she could speak, her grandmother broke in.

"Now, you listen, Jim. I watched that game, and the other girls were flat-out scared. You can't blame Laurie. She's only a fifth grader. You put too much pressure on her."

Laurie couldn't believe her ears. Grandma was sticking up for her!

"I'm sorry, Laurie," Coach Preston said gently. "Your grandmother is right. We have to be patient and let the other girls settle in."

Laurie felt she needed to settle down. She remembered how peaceful Maggie had looked as she sat knitting with Grandma.

"Grandma, after we clean up from supper, could you teach me to knit?" Laurie askcd.

A smile lit up Grandma's face. "Of course, dear. I think you'll like it."

When she'd first arrived at Compton Middle School, Laurie had felt like a nobody walking the halls. Now it seemed that the wholc student body knew her—and she would have given anything to go back to being unknown.

Dawn and Jackie must have spread the word about the outcome of the game. Worse yet, they must have told everyone what Mr. Riley had said, because Laurie had earned a nickname. Kids she didn't even know greeted her with "Hi, Gunner!"

It was so unfair. Laurie went outside to find Howard. She could count on him to be sympathetic. She heard two boys taunt her again as she walked down the school steps.

"Hey, Gunner, nice game!"

Laurie looked up and saw Howard's tormentors, Butch and Eddie. Even they knew about the game, and they had been out of town playing for the boys' team. To make things worse, the boys had won their game by twenty points.

"Did your boyfriend keep track of all those shots on his laptop?" Eddie laughed.

"That might have caused a meltdown," Butch said. Then he added, "When you see How-weird, tell him we're looking for him."

Laurie glared at the boys as they left, then ducked under the evergreen branches. She found Howard sitting with his back against the trunk, scribbling away at his homework.

"Hey, Laurie," he said, "thanks for not telling those guys where I am. Sorry they were ragging on you."

"I hate this place, Howard," Laurie sighed. "First no one knew or cared who I was. Now everyone teases me."

"You guys will play better on Friday," Howard said. "It's an away game, so you won't have to worry about Dawn or Jackie or any of their snotty friends."

"Yeah," Laurie sighed, "all we'll have to worry about is getting slaughtered again."

If Coach Preston was discouraged that afternoon at practice, it didn't show. He had the girls sit in their circle, and he stood in the middle.

"We got stomped yesterday," he said. "It's over. Let's get

ready to win on Friday. The one thing that didn't happen out there yesterday was fun. Some of you girls looked as if you thought the world would end if you made a mistake."

He had the team stand, then handed Laurie a basketball. "Pass the ball around the circle. Pass behind your back, through your legs, any way you want. Just try to surprise the person you throw the ball to."

The girls started stiffly but soon warmed up. When the giggles began, Coach Preston gave Laurie a second ball. With two balls in play, there was lots of laughter.

"From now on, this is our first drill every day. Let's see how many balls we can work up to."

Laurie had a feeling that practice—and the team—was going to be a lot more fun from now on.

Chapter 5

Road Trip

Laurie felt good as she boarded the team bus on Friday afternoon for the game against the Newton Longhorns. If her dad was right when he said, "How you practice is how you'll play," she thought the Cyclones would play well.

The passing drill had loosened the girls up and made them more alert. They could handle three balls at once now, whizzing them around the circle. They planned to use the drill in their pregame warmups.

Playing a road game also seemed to help everyone relax. Dawn, Jackie, and their friends most likely wouldn't travel to Newton to watch the game, and if the Cyclones had as few fans as last time, maybe the team wouldn't be so uptight worrying about making mistakes.

Eileen and Shirley got on the bus together. Shirley smiled at Laurie as she walked toward the back. But Eileen stopped to talk to her.

"I'm sorry about my dad," she said, sitting next to Laurie.

Laurie could feel her face turn red just thinking about being called a gunner.

"It's not your fault," Laurie sighed. "I can't control my dad either. Will your father be at the game?"

"He's coming, but he's promised to be on his best behavior," Eileen reassured Laurie. "Anyway, I thought you played great."

"Thanks," Laurie said with a grin, and Eileen left to join Shirley.

The bus was ready to leave by the time Howard stumbled on board. He had his ever-present laptop tucked under one arm and several large sheets of poster board tucked under the other. He tripped on his shoelaces and sprawled in the aisle. After a moment, he checked that his laptop had survived another impact and then joined Laurie in her seat.

"Hi, Howard. What did you bring?" Laurie asked.

"Cheers. We're going to make some noise in the stands today, to give you guys encouragement."

"Howard, if you play those sound effects again without warning anyone, the parents may chase you out of the gym."

"I know, Laurie. Our fans aren't ready for that yet. That's why I'm starting simple, with posters."

The bus ride lasted forty-five minutes, and Laurie tried several times to sneak a look at Howard's signs. But he guarded them vigilantly. So she spent most of the ride admiring the view. Newton was in the middle of farm country, and the land reminded her of Bradley.

By the time they piled off the bus, Laurie was feeling homesick. She wished she could be with Christy and was eager to take her mind off her homesickness by playing ball.

The pregame warmups went well. Laurie started with one ball, and Howard flipped her another each time she nodded. Soon there were three basketballs flying around the circle, and the girls were loose and laughing. The Compton parents gave the team a round of applause.

Coach Preston stuck to the same lineup that had started the opening game: Laurie and Wheezy at guard, Maggie in the middle, and Jesse and Angela up front.

The Newton center won the tip, but this time the Cyclones got back on defense and prevented the Longhorns from scoring, so no damage was done. Laurie hit a jump shot early and forced Newton to play her tightly, which enabled Laurie to dribble around her defender and create some excellent scoring opportunities for the Cyclones.

The problem was that the Cyclones weren't hitting their shots. Maggie made one basket when a rebound bounced to her and she shot before she had time to think. She missed several other shots, her face turning a bright red with each one.

Jesse had the worst luck. She shot three balls that spun around the rim and off. They could have easily dropped through for baskets, but they didn't.

Angela and Wheezy needed a rest after playing half the quarter. Both had been guarding active players who kept them running every second on defense.

The quarter ended with the Cyclones down, but only by a score of 10 to 6. The team was gaining confidence.

Howard had been surprisingly quiet. Then as the second quarter began, Laurie was called for a foul. She had nearly blocked a shot, but her hand had slid off the ball and onto the arm of the Newton player. The loud slap had made it an easy call for the referee.

As the players lined up for the foul shot, Howard came down in front of the Compton bleachers and held up a sign. He shouted, "B - E - A - T! Beat Mooton!" at the top of his lungs. Then he pushed a button on his laptop, and a drawn-out MOOOOOOOO! echoed throughout the gym.

The Newton fans booed. The Compton fans laughed but didn't join Howard when he repeated his cheer. Coach Preston waved his arm at him to stop, and Howard scrambled back onto the bleachers.

Despite Howard's posters (which read, "Cream Mooton!" "Compton Is Butter Than Mooton!" "Dear Dairy, Compton's Going to Win!") and dozens of computerized moos, the Cyclones trailed at the half 23 to 12.

Coach Preston took out Wheezy and Angela at the end of the second quarter to give them a solid twenty-minute rest during the halftime break. He started the second half playing Laurie, Wheezy, Li, Angela and Eileen. The Cyclones might have been giving away height at every position, but they had their quickest team on the floor.

Coach Preston told Li and Laurie to press each time the Newton team brought the ball up court. Wheezy and Angela were to lurk near midcourt. They would try to trap the ball if a Newton player got it past Laurie and Li. Eileen would be left by herself to defend the basket.

Had Newton been a more experienced team, they would have thrown long passes, and Eileen would soon have been in foul trouble as she tried to defend the basket. But instead, the Longhorns' guards panicked under Laurie and Li's pressure. Li darted around the court like a dragonfly, deflecting passes with her arms and legs. Like her namesake, Larry Bird, Laurie was an expert at guessing where a harried player would throw the ball. Time and again, the Longhorns would throw a pass only to have Li tip it or Laurie pick it off.

Soon the desperate Longhorns started fouling. And if Li were a stronger shooter, the Cyclones might have caught up. As it was, though, she made only two free throws out of six tries from the line, and the third quarter ended with the score 27 to 23. The Cyclones were within four points.

Once again, Laurie heard Mr. Riley bellowing over the other voices in the crowd, but this time he sounded happy. The Cyclones were playing as a team, and his Eileen was a part of it.

Unfortunately, pressing for an entire half with only eight players was too much to ask of the Cyclones. In the fourth quarter, the team grew tired and began to foul. The Longhorns didn't waste their opportunities. They made eight foul shots in the fourth quarter and won by a score of 39 to 31.

Laurie wasn't happy to lose another game, but she felt good about the progress the team had made since Monday. The Newton Longhorns had been forced to give their all to come away with a victory. When Coach Preston started a chorus of "We Are the Champions" on the bus ride home, none of the girls felt foolish for joining in.

Leadership

The Cyclones practiced on Saturday morning. Coach Preston didn't push them hard, since most of the girls were feeling the effects of their all-out effort the day before. Only Li and Laurie seemed to have their usual energy.

When they finished running laps and headed for the locker room, Li asked Laurie a favor.

"If you don't have to leave right away, could you help me with my foul shots? I felt bad missing those four yesterday. If I had made a couple more, we could have really put the pressure on Newton."

Laurie beamed. Nothing made her happier than helping a teammate who wanted to improve.

"Sure I'll help," she told Li. "But don't blame yourself for yesterday. We never would have come close to them without you."

Thirty minutes later, when Coach Preston was ready to leave, both girls were smiling. Laurie had shown Li how to spin the ball off her fingers to give her shots a better chance of dropping in the basket. Li was catching on quickly and was beginning to feel comfortable on the foul line.

"We'll shoot together after every practice until your new stroke becomes a habit," Laurie said.

"What are you doing the rest of the day?" Li asked.

"Nothing much. Probably fooling around on my computer," Laurie answered.

"We could go to the movies," Li suggested. "If you want to, that is," she added with a shrug.

"My dad can drop us off at the mall," Laurie said, grinning broadly.

It wasn't until she was in bed that night that Laurie realized she hadn't thought of Christy once that day.

The snow and ice had melted, so on Sunday morning, Laurie and her father went on their customary jog. Laurie dribbled down the empty sidewalks, breathing in the crisp air. The pounding of her dribble echoed in the still morning.

Suddenly, she heard another ball bouncing. She turned to see Li coming up fast behind her. When they reached the middle school parking lot, she and Laurie raced side by side, pushing each other to go faster without losing the ball.

As they passed through the sleepy Compton neighborhoods, more of the Cyclone players heard the basketballs dribbling and joined the parade. By the time the Prestons got back to their own street, the whole team was with them.

Grandma was sweeping her new front steps when she heard the noise. She caught Laurie's eye and smiled at the sight of her son followed by eight girls bouncing basketballs. Naturally, she invited everyone in for breakfast.

On Monday morning the kids were still calling Laurie "Gunner." She decided to try a new approach. Instead of looking hassled, she forced herself to smile and say hello. It was worth the effort just to see the disappointed looks on her tormentors' faces.

At lunch time, Dawn and Jackie were leaving the cafeteria as Laurie walked in. They pretended not to see her. Laurie told Howard when she joined him at a table, "Sometimes being ignored is the best you can hope for."

"Well, I hated it when our so-called fans ignored me," Howard grumbled. "Why wouldn't they try any of my cheers? I spent hours making those posters before the Newton game."

"It's not the posters, Howard. It's the team. We haven't done enough on the court to make our fans feel like cheering."

"Maybe you're right. I'm bringing my laptop today, but I'm not going to play any sound effects unless people ask me to," Howard promised.

That afternoon's game was another road game, this time in nearby Belair. Coach Preston was as optimistic as ever, and his relaxed, low-key attitude was just what the young Cyclones team needed to stay focused.

When the Cyclones filed into the Belair gym, they were met by the Bobcat manager, Jamie. As she led them to the locker room, she noticed Howard's laptop, and the two managers got into a discussion about computers. By the time the team reached the locker room, Jamie and Howard had exchanged e-mail addresses and made plans to play chess over the Internet.

After Jamie left, Howard told Laurie he'd learned some useful information, too. The Belair coach had seen Millbrook rout the Cyclones last week. She expected her team to win easily today. Howard suspected the Bobcats felt they wouldn't need to play hard to win the game. Maybe the improved Cyclones would take the Bobcats by surprise.

The Bobcat fans gave the Cyclones a friendly cheer when they ran their passing drill. As usual, the Cyclones had few fans of their own, so the encouragement was welcome.

Once the game began, however, the cheers were all for the Bobcats. The Belair team came out confident and loose. They scored a couple of easy baskets.

Then Laurie noticed that the girl guarding Jesse was no match for her under the boards. Jesse tore one rebound right out of her hands. So Laurie concentrated on getting the ball to Jesse.

Jesse scored twice, pushing her way past her defender. On the second shot, she was fouled. When she made the free throw, the Cyclones led for the first time all season, 5 to 4.

The Bobcats expected Laurie to shoot every time the Cyclones had possession. But in the week since their disastrous opening game, Laurie's teammates had begun to look for the ball.

Time and again, Laurie was double-teamed. Angela, Jesse, and even Maggie cut for the hoop the second their defenders left them to guard Laurie. Laurie fed them perfect passes, and the Cyclones made the baskets needed to keep up with their taller opponents. At halftime, the Bobcats led but only by a score of 23 to 21.

The Cyclones were sky high in the locker room, and Coach Preston had to calm them down. His main concern was that Angela and Wheezy had three fouls each; if either committed just two more, she would be disqualified.

"Ladies, you played a great half, but there's a long way to go. The Bobcats were overconfident. Now they know we can play. They'll be tougher this half. Stay calm, stay close, and we'll try to steal a victory."

Laurie could tell her dad wanted to win. He had forgotten to tell the Cyclones to have fun.

As soon as she brought the ball up court to start the second half, Laurie saw that the Bobcats had changed their strategy. She reached the top of the key, and there was no sign of a double-team.

Laurie thought she could get her shot off, but she would

rather pass. She could still hear the chant "Gunner! Gunner! Gunner!" and remembered the sick feeling it had given her.

She passed the ball to Wheezy, who swung it to Jesse. Jesse tried to find Maggie under the hoop, but her pass was tipped, and the Bobcats came up with the ball. The player Jesse was guarding beat her down the floor for an easy lay-up.

The pattern held throughout the third quarter. Laurie didn't shoot unless she was wide open. The Cyclones repeatedly passed the ball until they turned it over. The quarter ended with the score a disappointing 32 to 25.

As the fourth quarter began, one of the Bobcats chased a loose ball toward the Cyclone bench. Grandma had her knitting spread out on the bleacher beside her front-row seat. As the Bobcat player saved the ball, her leg got tangled around a strand of blue yarn. She turned to run down court and took a nasty spill.

The angry girl ripped the yarn from her leg and rushed over to the bleachers. Grandma had been about to apologize when the girl ripped the knitting from her hands, threw it on the floor, and stomped on it.

"Crazy old lady!" she shrieked. "Keep your junk out of the way before someone breaks a leg!"

Everyone in the gym was stunned into silence.

Psycho

The Belair coach and the referee arrived at that moment. They led the player, who wore number "8" on her Bobcats jersey, to her own bench. A time-out was called to let tempers cool.

Grandma sat with her face in her hands. She seemed embarrassed that she had caused the accident and shocked that the player had yelled at her. Howard picked up her knitting, which was soiled from being stomped on.

Coach Preston gathered his team. He planned to use this free time-out to set up a press. Maggie and Laurie sat on each side of Grandma, comforting her.

Coach Preston called, "Maggie, guard number 11. We're pressing."

To the amazement of all, Maggie growled, "No, Coach. I have number 8."

Laurie saw the fire in Maggie's eyes, and her dad must have, too, for he said, "Angela, you take number 11. Play hard, girls."

Coach Preston sent out Laurie, Li, Angela, Wheezy, and Maggie. Number 8 waited at the sidelines to inbound the ball for Belair. Maggie leaped up and down in front of her, spinning her arms like a windmill.

Twice the ball deflected off Maggie and out of bounds. The third time, Maggie tipped it along the sidelines, and Laurie grabbed it. She spotted Li streaking up court. Laurie wound up and threw a perfect baseball pass that Li caught in full stride. She dribbled once and scored.

The Cyclones pressed again. This time a different Bobcat inbounded. Maggie chased Number 8 around the court, flailing her arms, daring the Bobcats to pass the ball into her area.

Laurie and Li double-teamed the Belair guard in the backcourt. The desperate Bobcat ball handler leaped and lobbed a long pass over her teammates' outstretched arms. Wheezy intercepted the pass and whipped it to Li. Li found Laurie along the baseline for another basket.

The Bobcats' coach had seen enough. She called a time-out, which gave the Cyclone substitutes and Howard a chance to leap from the bench and swarm their team.

"Maggie, you're psycho!" Howard yelled, hugging the girl who towered over him. "You're all psychos!"

Jesse, Eileen, and Shirley picked up the chant. "Psychos! Psychos!" they yelled, stomping their feet and facing the bleachers.

The two rows of Compton fans took up the cry. "Psychos! Psychos!" they chanted. With each cheer, they stomped the bleachers until the structure shook.

The referee had to wave the teams back on the floor to resume play, because the fans' cheering had drowned out the buzzer.

The shocked Bobcats crept back onto the court. They were reluctant to inbound the ball against this group of maniacs.

Maggie guarded Number 8, who tried to find a safe place to throw the ball. Maggie's windmilling arms blocked the Bobcat player's view, and Number 8 hesitated until the referee's whistle blew. The Bobcats had failed to put the ball in play within five seconds. Cyclone ball!

Maggie threw the ball to Li, who passed to Laurie. Gunner or no gunner, Laurie was psyched. She dribbled once and launched a three pointer. The ball split the cords, and the Psycho Cyclones led 35 to 34.

Laurie's shot seemed to take something out of both teams. As the clock wound down to three minutes, neither team could capitalize on its opportunities. Then Laurie hit a lay-up for the

Cyclones, and the beleaguered Number 8 managed to tip in a shot missed by one of her teammates.

With twelve seconds left in the game, Wheezy fouled one of the Bobcats in the act of shooting. It was Wheezy's fifth foul, putting her out of the game. She hugged her teammates and begged them to hang on and win.

The Bobcat player stepped to the line. Coolly ignoring Howard's screams, she sunk both shots. The Bobcats led 38 to 37.

Coach Preston waved to Laurie, and she called the Cyclones' last time-out. Wheezy, Shirley, and Eileen jumped off the bench and greeted their teammates with hugs and shouts of encouragement. Howard was so eager to hear Coach Preston's plan that he had to be reminded to pass around water and towels.

Coach Preston stayed cool. He knelt in front of the bench and spoke. "Laurie, bring the ball to the top of the key. At five seconds, I'll whistle. Try to drive. If you get stuck, look for Jesse in the corner or Maggie under the hoop."

Li inbounded, and Laurie dribbled deliberately up court. She circled near the top of the key, protecting the ball from the Bobcat defenders. Just when she was convinced she must have missed the signal, she heard her father's whistle pierce the noise from the crowd.

Laurie faked right, put the ball behind her back, and drove left. She took two steps and then leaped into the air. A huge hand rose along with her, determined to block her shot. Laurie adjusted herself in midair and flipped the ball underneath the defender's arm.

The ball rose, rested for a second on the front of the rim, and spun through the net. Laurie crashed to the floor, so focused on her shot that she neglected to break her fall.

Before she could decide whether she was hurt, she was at the bottom of a pile of squirming, hugging, shouting Cyclones. The team had its first victory.

Chapter 6

Teammates

The Compton fans poured onto the floor to join the fun. The Belair faithful filed out as the celebration went on. Coach Preston announced that the team would stop for pizza—his treat.

On the bus ride home, Howard beat the keys of his laptop unmercifully. After all his efforts to generate cheers, he had done it by accident. The fans loved the nickname "Psychos" because it so accurately described the way Maggie and the others scrambled across the court: arms waving frantically and bodies straining, stopping the opponents in their tracks. Laurie noticed he was now typing ideas for new cheers.

By the time the bus got to the Slice of Life Pizzeria, most of the parents who had been at the game were there. As Laurie, Li, and Howard walked in the door, they were greeted by the chant "Psychos! Psychos! Psychos!" Other patrons, who must have been treated to a description of the game by the excited fans, joined in the cheer.

The occupants of one booth, however, remained stubbornly silent. In a far corner, wolfing down their pizza so they could leave, sat Dawn, Jackie, and the twins.

When Coach Preston came in after his mother, the cheers grew louder. He waved his thanks and slid into a booth with Laurie, Li, and Howard.

Before the noise had completely died, the kitchen doors were thrown open. A short, stocky man, dressed in white and carrying the biggest pizza Laurie had ever seen, headed for their table.

"Congratulations, Jim, from one old Cyclone to another!" he said, setting the pizza in the middle of their table.

"Ralph, you old rascal!" Coach Preston yelled, jumping up to hug the man. "Everyone, this is my old backcourt mate, Ralph Wilson."

Introductions were made, and Ralph squeezed in next to his friend. Laurie couldn't take her eyes off the pizza, which was hot and fresh. Each slice was covered with different toppings. She spun the pan until she found a slice with her favorites, eggplant and basil.

Ralph's crew took orders from the other Cyclones. Someone selected "We Are the Champions" on the jukebox. Coach Preston and his old teammate stood and led everyone in song, while Dawn and her friends slunk out the door.

"Your dad and I sang that song the night we beat Millbrook for the county championship," Ralph told Laurie. "As long as I own a jukebox, that tune will be on it."

Laurie got home late and was exhausted from the excitement and the game. But she couldn't go to bed without e-mailing Christy.

To: 2Christy@hitech.com
From: LBP@hitech.com
We won! At last we won a game! Our press was great, and we beat Belair 39 to 38. Can you guess who made the winning basket?
Hope you're still undefeated!
Laughing-Out-Loud Laurie

Tuesday's practice was light. Coach Preston would have canceled it altogether, but the Cyclones had their next game on Friday, and he wanted them to be as well prepared as possible.

The girls walked through some drills, talked strategy, and shot free throws. Coach gave them a pep talk as they sat in a circle. Friday's game would be a home game, the first since their humiliating season opener.

"Bring the same spirit and desire to Friday's game as you did to the last," he said, "and you'll have nothing to be ashamed of, win or lose."

Laurie was sure everyone on the team got the message.

Homecoming

"What a difference a win makes!" Laurie said to Howard.

Howard grinned. Every person they met as they walked the halls of Compton Middle School had something good to say to Laurie.

"Psycho Gunner, great game Monday night!"

"Hey, Gunner, stomp Bingham today."

"We'll be there this afternoon, Gunner!"

Even though the kids were still calling Laurie "Gunner," the new tone gave the nickname a whole different meaning. Laurie felt she had finally earned some respect. She hoped her teammates would play as fearlessly today as they had on Monday.

According to Howard, who had used his contacts on the Internet to get information on Bingham, the Bears were two and one so far this season. Their best player was their center,

Tawana Johnson. At five feet eleven, she was an inch taller than Maggie and was a terror on the boards. The rest of the Bears concentrated on getting the ball to Tawana, since she scored most of their points.

As Laurie led the team up the stairs and onto the court, a cheer broke out from the stands. She thought the Cyclones were in the wrong gym. Howard cued his storm sound effects, and the fans joined in, shouting, "Howl, Cyclones, howl!" It sounded to Laurie as if every kid in the school was there.

"Well, almost every kid. I'll bet Dawn and Jackie aren't around," she thought.

Upon closer inspection, Laurie noticed that really only one section of the bleachers was full. But the size of this crowd was a big improvement over the few fans at their first home game.

When the team formed a circle and started its passing drill, the crowd erupted with noise. "Psychos! Psychos! Psychos!" the fans chanted. Urged on by the support, the Cyclones threw their sharpest passes and kept three basketballs spinning around the ring.

By the opening tip, the Bingham Bears were intimidated by the raucous crowd. They played cautiously, knowing that the least mistake would cue more thunderous cheering from the Cyclones' side of the gym.

The Bingham defender was a little shorter than Laurie, so Laurie was confident she could get her shot off. She faked a pass to Maggie and went up for a jumper. The shot hit nothing but net, and the Cyclones were on the scoreboard.

At the quarter, the Cyclones led 14 to 8, and Laurie had scored eight points. The Bingham coach made a switch in the backcourt, taking out the girl who had been guarding Laurie. The substitute was an even shorter girl, but she quickly showed that she was not bothered by the noisy crowd. She kept up with Laurie's every move.

Each time up court, the new player worked her dribble until she could get a pass to Tawana. Maggie tried valiantly to keep Tawana away from the basket, but she was overmatched. When she fronted Tawana, the guard lobbed a pass over Maggie's head that Tawana easily caught. When Maggie played behind her, Tawana shot over Maggie. By halftime, the game was tied at 26. Maggie and Eileen had three fouls each, all drawn while guarding Tawana.

Coach Preston used the halftime to set up his press. He put Jesse on Tawana. Maybe her big body would force Tawana farther from the basket. He assigned Li to guard a player who seemed reluctant to shoot; chances were good Bingham wouldn't pass the ball to that player often, and Li could drop down court and help Jesse. Laurie and Wheezy would chase the ball, while Angela would hang back under the basket.

Laurie held her breath as the second half started. She knew that if the press didn't work, the Cyclones would give up a slew of lay-ups. They had to win today, while the fans were on their side. If the team disappointed them, they might never come back.

The Bingham Bears had the ball to start the second half. When the Cyclones set up their press, the Compton fans went wild. Jesse couldn't windmill her arms as effectively as Maggie could, so Tawana managed to get the ball inbounds. But when one of the Bears' guards threw the ball back to Tawana, Jesse tore the pass away. She found Laurie scooting along the base line and passed her the ball for a quick two points.

Howard started the "Psychos!" chant. The fans stood and howled, their feet stomping the bleachers in rhythm.

Tawana threw a long pass up court. Two Bingham players bore down on Angela, who was alone under the basket. Laurie knew that if Angela tried to stop the dribbler, the girl would flip the ball to her teammate for a lay-up. But if Angela guarded the free girl instead, the ball handler would drive all the way to the hoop.

Angela waved her arms and let out a piercing scream. The ball bounced off the startled dribbler's knee and flew out of bounds. The Cyclones had possession.

Li inbounded to Laurie. Laurie dribbled smoothly, shaking the defender who met her at midcourt. She drove straight at Tawana. Poised to spring, Tawana went for Laurie's fake. The tall girl leaped, and Laurie flipped the ball to Jesse.

Jesse snatched the pass and, keeping her body between the ball and any defenders, banged it home. In another minute, the Cyclones had scored the first eight points of the quarter.

The Bingham Bears called a time-out.

Coach Preston put the Cyclones back in their regular defense. He sent Maggie and Shirley in for Angela and Wheezy, who were breathing hard.

The teams traded baskets for the rest of the quarter. Jesse played between Tawana and the basket. Li left the girl she was guarding and tried to tip away passes thrown in front of Tawana.

The Cyclones couldn't keep Tawana from getting the ball, but they were making it more difficult for her to shoot. Soon she was missing more baskets than she was making.

The fourth quarter began with the Cyclones ahead 36 to 30. Coach Preston set up the press one more time, and again the Cyclones shut down the Bears. Their offense was on the mark. Li scored on two fast breaks, Maggie made two shots off Jesse's misses, and with twenty seconds left in the game, the Cyclones were ten points ahead.

Laurie dribbled away from frustrated Bears while time wound down, then threw the ball straight up in the air as the buzzer sounded. Before it came down, Li had wrapped her arms around Laurie. The fans cheered long and loud while the Cyclones hugged one another and Coach Preston. Their record was even, and they had won the hearts of their fans.

Appeal Play

By the time the Cyclones arrived at the Slice of Life, the place was packed. Ralph waved to Laurie and Howard. They pushed through the crowd to a big round table in the back. A sign hanging over it read "Cyclone Zone."

"I hear it was a great game!" Ralph said to Laurie. "Is your dad coming?"

Laurie smiled her thanks. "I think so. He told Howard he'd meet us here."

Laurie wondered where her father was. It wasn't like him to leave without her, even though Slice of Life was within walking distance of the school. And since he had left before she did, why wasn't he here? Even if he had given Grandma a ride home, he should have been here by now.

Ralph kept bringing pizzas and pitchers of soda until the Cyclones were stuffed. Most of the fans had left, many of them stopping to congratulate the players on their way out.

Li was about to leave with her parents when Ralph stopped them at the door. Laurie saw Mr. and Mrs. Tang nod their heads. Then Li came back to the team table.

"Laurie, your father just called. He wants us all to wait here for a team meeting," Li said.

The girls looked at one another, then at Howard.

"Don't look at me," Howard said. "I never know what's going on in that man's head."

The suspense lasted another five minutes. Then Coach Preston came through the swinging kitchen doors.

"This is getting weirder and weirder. Why didn't he come in the front door?" Laurie asked Howard.

Before Howard could answer, Dawn and Jackie followed Coach Preston into the dining room. Laurie's jaw dropped. She glanced around the table and saw that the other girls looked equally shocked. For the first time all night, Maggie's face turned red.

"Cyclones," Coach Preston said, "I'd like to call this meeting to order. These young ladies would like to address the squad."

He motioned for Dawn and Jackie to step forward. Embarrassed, they stared at the menu board on the wall rather than make eye contact with their former teammates.

At last, Dawn spoke. "Jackie and I want to say we're sorry. We know we teased you guys too much."

Jackie looked at the ceiling and said, "Congratulations on your two wins. We never thought you could do it without us."

Coach Preston put one of his big hands on Dawn's shoulder and one on Jackie's. "Now comes the hard part," he told them.

Jackie sighed, "We know we didn't work hard enough at practice. We'd like to come back to the team."

Dawn added, "We'll understand if you don't want us, but we think the Cyclones would be great this year if we were back on the team."

"I told the girls," Coach Preston said, "that we would need time to think things over. Would anyone object to giving Dawn and Jackie our decision after practice tomorrow?"

Laurie looked around the table. Her teammates seemed as taken aback as she was. Things were going so well for the Cyclones without Dawn and Jackie. Would all that disappear if they allowed Dawn and Jackie to rejoin? But how many games could Compton win without them? And what if someone got hurt? Could the team expect to make it through the season with only eight players?

"How about the twins?" Jesse asked. "Do they want to come back, too?"

"No," Dawn answered. "They love volleyball. Jackie and I don't mind it, but we feel as if we're missing out every time you guys play without us."

"All I want is another chance to show you the kind of player I can be," Jackie said.

"We practice from ten until noon tomorrow," Coach Preston told them. "If you come to the gym at twelve, I'll give you the team's decision."

When Laurie got home, she shot up to the spare room and her computer. She was hoping to chat with Christy and get her advice. She logged on and saw that she had e-mail.

To: LBP@hitech.com
From: 2Christy@hitech.com
What do you know? The Bucs are 4 and 0! Wish you were here for the fun. Hope you won your game. Talk to you soon.
Can't-Miss Christy

It was late, and Christy must have gone to bed by now. Laurie sent her an e-mail that she hoped Christy would read first thing in the morning.

To: 2Christy@hitech.com
From: LBP@hitech.com
Undefeated, wow! We won our game, too. But big problems, and I need your advice. If you're on-line at 9:00 tomorrow morning, maybe you can go to a chat room with me.
Lost-in-Thought Laurie

Would Dawn and Jackie make the Cyclones stronger? Or would they destroy the team's chemistry and ruin the season for everyone? Suppose the Cyclones refused to take them back, and one or two players got hurt? Then what? Tired as she was, it was a long time before Laurie fell asleep.

Comeback

Laurie checked her computer every half-hour until it was time to leave for practice. She wasn't surprised that there wasn't a message from Christy. Christy liked to sleep late on Saturdays, and even if she had practice, she wouldn't get up until the last minute.

Over breakfast, Laurie hoped her dad would give her his opinion on Dawn and Jackie. But instead he talked about the weather, the stories in the newspaper—any topic except the Cyclones. When Grandma congratulated Laurie on last night's win, Laurie thought she had her chance to bring up the Cyclones' problem. But then Grandma took up her knitting and started chatting with her son about household matters.

Laurie didn't know what to do. She wished her father would make the decision. Did he want Dawn and Jackie back so that he could have a better team? Or was he glad they were gone? Laurie stared at him, but she couldn't read the answer in his face.

The last time the Cyclones had practiced after a game, Coach Preston had gone easy on them. Today, however, he ran them ragged. Laurie and Li, usually the most energetic players, were so whipped that they leaned on each other during a time-out. But as tired as they were, the girls couldn't forget the big decision.

"Do you want them back?" Li asked Laurie.

"I don't know," Laurie answered honestly. "We could really use their scoring. But it seems like we weren't a team until they left. How about you?"

"I'm afraid your father will forget about me if they play," Li said. "It's easier for you. You'll be a starter anyway."

"Li, we couldn't win without you, not with three Dawns and four Jackies. My dad knows that," Laurie said. "And suppose Dawn wants to play point guard? That's my best position."

The girls had neither the time nor the breath for more talk as Coach Preston ran them through drills and a scrimmage. At twenty minutes past eleven, he sent them to shoot foul shots. Once Howard had recorded the results, the Cyclones gathered in a circle.

Coach Preston stood in the middle, slowly turning to make eye contact with each of the eight Cyclones.

"Ladies, I know you've given a lot of thought to whether to allow Dawn and Jackie to rejoin the team. Let's talk about the plusses and minuses for a few minutes. Then you can vote."

Jesse's hand slowly went up. "We could use two more players. By the end of the games, we're exhausted, even though we've trained hard."

"Any other plusses?" Coach Preston asked.

"They're good players, especially Dawn," Eileen volunteered. "I saw a few of the games last year, and she's a great shooter. We're bound to win more games with them than without."

"Not if they play like they did before," Li snapped. "They hogged the ball, and the whole offense bogged down."

"I guess we've moved to the minuses. Who else would like to speak?" Coach Preston asked.

"There should be no teasing," said Maggie, her dark eyes flashing. "I put up before, but now I prove that I belong."

Jesse spoke again. "They teased me plenty about my weight last year, and I hated it. Well, I've worked to get in shape. Have they? They goofed off at practice, and who knows what they were doing while we worked out over the holidays."

Laurie felt she had to say something. She had been picturing the Dawn and Jackie who had spoiled her first weeks in Compton. Maybe there was a compromise.

"How about if we let them back on a trial basis?" Laurie suggested. "If after a week, Coach doesn't think they're working hard enough or doesn't think they're being good teammates, they're off the team for good."

The girls thought this over, then began nodding. Even Li, who was the most afraid of losing playing time, thought the idea was fair. She squeezed Laurie's hand.

"Does anyone object to my telling Dawn and Jackie that they're back on the team, effective Monday, but on a trial basis?" Coach Preston asked.

Laurie looked around at her teammates. No one raised any objections.

"Great! Don't forget practice on Monday and a home game against Parkside on Tuesday. Have a good weekend."

Laurie wondered if any of the girls could really relax this weekend knowing that their team would never be the same come Monday.

Full Strength

After catching a movie with Li, Laurie finally got to chat with Christy over the Internet on Saturday afternoon. It was too late to get Christy's help with her decision about letting Dawn and Jackie back on the team, but Christy seemed to think that Laurie had made the right choice.

"What's more fun than winning? It sounds like you need those two. You can't even have a decent practice with only eight players," she wrote.

The next day, Laurie tried to talk to Howard about the Cyclones' decision, but he wasn't any help.

"Hey, no one asked for my opinion. Your dad doesn't think of me as part of the team," he complained.

"Well, how would you feel if Butch and Eddie quit a team you were playing for and then wanted to come back?" Laurie asked.

"That's a no-brainer. I'd let them."

"Are they that good?"

"No, but they'd squash me like a bug if I voted against them."

Laurie smiled despite herself. At least Howard's opinion of the two boys was consistent.

At Monday's practice, there was some awkwardness during the passing drill, but Dawn and Jackie quickly learned the routine. Laurie wondered if the team could handle a fourth ball now that there were ten players.

Dawn and Jackie played with the second team, which made for a spirited scrimmage. Laurie had to play her best against Dawn, who was two inches taller than Laurie and was a good jumper. Once, when Dawn had anticipated Laurie's behind-the-back dribble, she'd stolen the ball.

Jackie gave Jesse a good workout up front, too. Jackie didn't have much range on her shot, but if she got the ball near the basket, she was hard to stop.

Laurie noticed that Dawn and Jackie tired quickly. Her dad

was working the girls hard, and the rest of the Cyclones were well conditioned compared to the newcomers. Laurie hoped the two girls could get into shape in time to help the team.

On Tuesday, Laurie led the Cyclones up the stairs to face another noisy crowd. As soon as she dribbled over the end line, the fans began chanting, "Psychos! Psychos! Psychos!" Their cheering even temporarily drowned out Howard's sound effects.

Parkside's style of play reminded Laurie of the Cyclones' at the start the season: the Ponies were hesitant and made poor decisions. But playing well against a bad team proved difficult for the Cyclones. The Ponies turned the ball over so often that the Cyclones found themselves running, gunning, and making mistakes of their own.

Howard got the crowd involved early. He held up posters that read, "Are the Ponies Going to Beat Us?" After the crowd yelled the words, he hit a key on his laptop. The answer was a loud computerized "Neigh!"

Thanks to some clutch shooting from Laurie and Angela, the Cyclones were up by ten points at the half. Dawn and Jackie would start the second half, after sitting on the bench for the first two quarters. Laurie would join Dawn in the backcourt, while Maggie and Jesse would play up front with Jackie.

The first time up court during the second half, the Cyclones turned the ball over. Both Jesse and Jackie cut across the lane at the same time, but both missed Laurie's pass, and the ball bounced over the end line.

But for the most part, the girls played well together. With more firepower in the game, Maggie didn't have to look for shots.

Instead, she could concentrate on rebounding. She was at her best when scoring with her teammates' missed shots.

Jackie was a strong rebounder. With Jesse and Maggie also pounding the boards, Parkside got almost no second shots.

Laurie found it a luxury to have a fine shooter like Dawn as her backcourt mate. She was free to penetrate because she knew that if the inside was closed off, she could throw the ball out to Dawn, who more than likely would sink a jumper.

By the end of the third quarter, the Cyclones were ahead by sixteen points. During the last quarter, Coach Preston was able to pull out Maggie and Angela and give Shirley and Eileen some extended playing time. He even experimented with using Li at point guard. If Dawn resented not playing a single minute at her old position, she kept it to herself.

The Cyclones were able to keep their big lead without resorting to their deadly press. They played to hearty applause until the last two minutes, when the gym emptied out. The scoreboard read "Compton 43, Parkside 24."

Chapter 7

Transition

Gradually, Compton began to feel like home to Laurie. She couldn't pinpoint an exact date when she first felt this way, but now Bradley seemed just a place where she used to live.

When Laurie had first moved into Grandma's house, it had seemed strange to sit at the table for a meal. Now she would have felt odd if she grabbed her food and flopped in front of the TV.

Grandma herself had changed from a criticizing stranger to a person Laurie knew was on her side. And thanks to Grandma's warmth, Laurie's teammates hung out at the house on weekends and holidays. Howard was there so often that Coach Preston joked about charging him rent.

Laurie realized that she sometimes went for days without e-mailing Christy. She missed Christy if she thought about her, but she was so busy with her new team and school that there was little time to feel lonely. Besides, now she had Li and Howard if she needed someone to talk to.

Christy must have felt the same way, because when they did chat, she didn't complain about missing Laurie. Christy's big news was that the Buccaneers were nine and zero and needed just one more win for an undefeated season.

The only Cyclones who never visited the Preston house were Dawn and Jackie. They no longer tormented their teammates and they worked hard at practice, but they kept to themselves outside the gym.

But their presence on the court had paid off in a major way. As Dawn and Jackie got into shape and worked their way into the starting lineup, the Cyclones became a powerful team. Their record improved to seven and two, and they weren't seriously challenged for weeks.

When the Newton Longhorns had come to Compton, the Cyclones easily won the rematch. And when Howard had played his computerized moos again, the home fans roared with laughter.

The final game of the season was on Valentine's Day against the Millbrook Tigers, the team that had humiliated Compton 41 to 16 in the season opener. Adding to the excitement was the fact that the Tigers were also seven and two. The winner of the game would be the league champion.

On the short bus ride to Millbrook, Laurie felt confident. The Cyclones were not the same team that had lost so badly on opening day. She almost felt sorry for Millbrook. How would they feel when a team they had routed ran all over them?

The importance of the game, and the fact that the schools were less than ten miles apart, guaranteed the biggest crowd either team had seen all season.

Laurie was right that the Cyclones had improved tremendously. But pregame warmups tipped her off that the Tigers seemed to have gotten better, too. The Tigers had developed a smooth passing drill of their own.

Her ears told her the Tigers' shooting had improved as well. During the shoot-around, the Millbrook end of the court was nearly silent; the ball didn't make much noise when it hit nothing but net.

Once the game started, the heaviest brick of a shot couldn't be heard because the Millbrook and Compton fans were fighting to outcheer each other. Laurie glanced at Howard, who was shaking his head in wonder and unplugging his speaker. No one could have heard his sound effects anyway.

Any illusions Laurie had entertained about this being an easy game were gone seconds into play. The Cyclones were stretched to the limit to stay even with the bigger, stronger Millbrook players.

Luckily, the Cyclones were on their game. Laurie and Dawn had the touch and scored whenever they were able to break free. Maggie, Jesse, and Jackie expended most of their energy defending and fighting for positions under the boards. Neither team could open more than a three-point lead, and the half ended with the score tied at 24.

As Laurie sat in the locker room, eating orange slices and catching her breath, she wondered if her father would call for the press. She wasn't sure that the Cyclones had the energy to make the defensive strategy work. Maggie, Dawn, and Jackie looked whipped. Jesse lay on a bench, a wet towel covering her eyes and forehead.

Coach Preston must have seen what Laurie did. At the start of the second half, he put the team in a zone defense and substituted players at nearly every whistle. Li seemed to be everywhere as a chaser in the zone, Angela and Wheezy took turns relieving the tired Cyclones under the basket, and the third quarter ended with the score tied at 33.

The Save

Howard took advantage of the relative quiet before the last quarter to begin the "Psychos" chant. Mr. Riley added his booming bass to the cheer. Li, still full of energy, bounced up and down in front of the Cyclones' bench. Laurie thought maybe these factors influenced Coach Preston, because he directed the Cyclones to set up their press. When the Cyclones' fans saw what the team was up to, they gave their loudest roar yet.

Maggie, the original Psycho, guarded against the inbound pass. Laurie and Dawn double-teamed the ball. Li played near midcourt, ready to dart in any direction to pursue a sloppy pass. Jesse waited back under the basket, her fierce scowl daring the Tigers to drive the lane.

The Millbrook coach countered with her five tallest players. Maggie forced a couple of turnovers, but more often than not, the Tigers succeeded in passing the ball over the heads of the shorter Cyclones. Millbrook was well prepared for the "Psycho Press."

For every easy basket the Cyclones scored off a steal, the Tigers broke the press and scored a lay-up. When Jesse picked up her fourth foul with two minutes left, Coach Preston pulled her out of the game and called off the press.

The Tigers called a time-out with the score 43 to 40 in Millbrook's favor. The Cyclones flopped on the bench to hear Coach Preston's advice. Laurie's legs felt like rubber, and her calves burned. She was grateful that she didn't drop the water bottle Howard flipped to her. She felt too tired to pick it up if she had dropped it.

When play resumed, the Tigers' center was on the line to shoot two foul shots. She missed the first, and Coach Preston called a time-out. This gave the girls another minute to rest, and Laurie could feel her energy coming back.

The Tiger players were exhausted, too. They were slumped over with their hands resting on their knees. They led by four points after their center made the second foul shot. But Laurie found Li on a fast break, and Li sunk a basket that brought the Cyclones within two. Both teams missed opportunities, and with ten seconds left, Millbrook led by two points.

Coach Preston used his final time-out to set up a play. In the last-second win over Belair, Laurie had driven to the hoop when the clock wound down to five seconds. The Cyclones would try the same play again, with Dawn staying on the perimeter in case Laurie was stopped.

Against Belair, Coach Preston had whistled to signal Laurie to start her drive. He couldn't take a chance on being heard in this madhouse. Laurie would have to use her own judgment as to when to shoot.

The play went sour right away. Dawn inbounded, but Laurie was double-teamed. She managed to pass the ball to Jackie, who got it across midcourt. When Jackie tried to pass the ball back to Laurie, it was deflected by one of the Millbrook players.

Laurie watched helplessly as seconds ticked away, and the ball bounced from player to player. One of the Tigers managed to grab the ball, but Jackie knocked it from her hands. The ball flew toward the end line with Laurie in hot pursuit.

Laurie dove, her arm fully extended. Her fingertips found

the ball as she crossed the end line. She flipped the ball over her shoulder.

Laurie crashed to the floor, skidding behind the basket. She twisted her body around in time to see Dawn launch a three-point shot. The ball left her fingertips an instant before the buzzer sounded.

The crowd fell silent. All eyes followed the long arcing shot, which reached its apex, seemed to hang for a moment, then headed for the rim.

When the ball split the net, Laurie leapt up, her bruises and fatigue forgotten. The Cyclones' fans swarmed the players. Grandma threw her skein of blue yarn up in the air. It cascaded over the crowd like silly string.

The Cyclones were the league champs!

Invitation

When the freshly showered girls came out of the locker room, Howard was waiting for them. He was so hoarse from rooting for the Cyclones that he had trouble making himself understood. At last, he made the players understand that Coach Preston wanted to talk to them and had asked that they wait in the bleachers.

Laurie sat with Li, huge smiles stretching across both their faces. As Dawn, Jackie, and the others joined them, they stared at the scoreboard, which still showed that wonderful final score. Laurie knew each of them would always remember this game.

When all ten players were there, Howard trotted over to the Millbrook coach's office, where Coach Preston had been using the telephone. Laurie hoped they weren't going to sing "We Are the Champions" right there in the other team's gym. That wouldn't be very sporting.

Soon Coach Preston and Howard stood in front of the bleachers. Laurie wondered what her father had to say.

"Congratulations, ladies, you played a wonderful game," he began. "You've earned a very special Presidents' Day weekend."

Laurie and Howard looked at each other. With all the excitement, Laurie had forgotten there was a three-day weekend coming up. What did her father mean about spending it in a special way?

"This year, for the first time, New York State is holding Middle School Championships. As a result of our win tonight, we've been invited to represent our league in the small-school tournament. Eight teams are invited, and by next Monday, one will be the state champion."

Laurie couldn't believe her ears. She and the other Cyclones jumped up and down and hugged one another.

"We'll leave for Albany right after school on Friday. The tournament starts on Saturday. If we win our game, we play on Sunday. If we win again, we play for the championship on Monday afternoon."

When the next round of screaming began to die down, Laurie waved to her dad. Coach Preston whistled for quiet and invited Laurie to speak.

"We qualified for this tournament by playing as a team," she said. "Let's go to Albany with ten equal members. All in favor of welcoming Dawn and Jackie back as full members of the squad, give a cheer!"

Roaring their approval, the girls took turns hugging Dawn

and Jackie, who were smiling so broadly, it looked painful. Then with arms still locked, the Cyclones headed for the bus.

Laurie was so excited that the rest of the night passed in a blur. She knew the bus ride had been noisy and filled with laughter. She could remember the cheer from the crowd when she and Li had walked into Slice of Life. But she couldn't remember what she'd eaten, what she'd said to people, or any other details.

It wasn't until the next morning, when Laurie saw that she had an e-mail from Christy, that she even thought to wonder what other schools were in the tournament.

To: LBP@hitech.com
From: 2Christy@hitech .com
Looks like 10 and 0 isn't enough for an undefeated season after all. We're invited to a tournament in Albany next weekend to name a state small-school champion! Any chance you and your dad could come see us play?
Cruising Christy

Laurie wasted no time to e-mail her best friend a reply.

To: 2Christy@hitech.com
From: LBP@hitech.com
Dad and I are coming to the tourney. Can't promise to watch you play, though. The Cyclones are in it, too! We beat Millbrook to win our league. Dawn sunk a three at the buzzer! Wouldn't it be something if we played against each other?????
Loving-It Laurie

Laurie leaned back and smiled. She'd give anything to see the look on Christy's face when she read that message.

Over breakfast, Laurie and Howard (who had just happened to stop by in time for Grandma's pancakes) learned more about the tournament.

"Dad," Laurie asked, "why didn't you tell us we had a chance to make the tournament?"

Coach Preston smiled. "I knew beating Millbrook was all the motivation you needed to play your hardest. Why worry about a state championship when we hadn't won our own league?"

"How's the tournament set up, Coach?" Howard asked.

"The eight schools will be seeded according to how well the tournament committee thinks they will do," Coach Preston explained. "The number one seed, the school most likely to win the tournament, will play number eight in the first round. Two plays seven, three plays six, and four and five play each other."

"That's just the way the colleges do it," Howard remarked, a drop of maple syrup hanging from his chin.

"What school will be number one, Dad?" Laurie asked.

"There's a good chance Bradley will be," he answered. "I don't think there are any other undefeated teams.

"What seed do you think we'll get?"

"I wish I knew, Laurie. I wish I knew."

Making a Stand

School on Monday was full of talk about the Cyclones. A state championship tournament would have been exciting at any time.

But during a cold, gloomy February, it was doubly welcome.

The boys' season was over. After their great start, they had suffered a few injuries, lost some close games, and ended up six and four. So the Psychos were the center of attention at Compton Middle School.

Mr. Riley arranged to charter a bus, with the Cyclone fans splitting the cost. Eileen was swamped with questions from kids who wanted to go to Albany for the weekend. She explained that no one could come without a parent. The seats were going quickly.

At lunch time, Howard and Laurie were discussing new cheers when Butch and Eddie came over to their table. Howard nervously checked that the lunchroom monitor, Mr. Landro, was within hailing distance. He slipped his laptop inside his jacket and zipped it up.

"Hey, Gunner!" Butch greeted Laurie.

Laurie ignored him. Eddie put his hand on Howard's shoulder.

"Hi, How-weird. Thanks for asking us to help manage the team this weekend. Our folks are busy, and unless we go on the team bus, we've got no way to get to Albany."

Howard's eyes got big. At last he stammered, "Sorry, Eddie, but Coach Preston won't let me bring anyone. I couldn't ask you guys if I wanted to."

"Are you sure, How-weird? Suppose you were too sick to go. Then maybe Butch and I could take your place," Eddie said.

"You know, you look kind of sick to me," Butch added.

Laurie looked at Howard, and he was starting to look sick. Would he let Butch and Eddie push him into staying home, after he had worked so hard all season?

Howard banged his spoon on the table, sending food flying from his tray. The noise drew everyone's attention.

"Everybody, listen up!" he yelled, his voice cracking.

Mr. Landro started walking over. Then he stopped to let Howard have his say. Butch and Eddie looked back and forth from Mr. Landro to Howard, not sure what was happening.

Howard stood and pushed his glasses back on his nose. With his voice shaking, he went on. "These two seventh graders have been bullying me all year. They kept me from managing the boys' team because I was afraid of them. Now they're trying to take my place managing the Psychos."

Laurie's teammates and lots of other kids who had enjoyed Howard's cheers started to boo. Butch and Eddie looked uneasy.

"I'm going to the state tournament on Friday," Howard yelled. "You may see me with a black eye or covered in garbage, but I'll be on that bus!"

The cafeteria rang with cheers for Howard. Laurie cheered louder than anyone. Butch and Eddie slunk away, careful to leave through the door farthest from Mr. Landro.

Howard smiled at Laurie, picked up his tray, and strode proudly across the cafeteria. He didn't even notice the orange Jell-O sliding down the front of his jacket.

Scouting

The two-hour bus ride up the New York State Thruway to Albany passed in no time. The team was noisy and excited, but the driver didn't mind. He said he'd graduated from Compton

Middle School himself and joined in when the team began singing "We Are the Champions."

Howard was using his laptop to get information on the Cyclones' first-round opponent. Compton had ended up with the fifth seed. This meant they would play the fourth-rated team, the Mohawk Marauders. So far, all Howard had learned was that the Marauders had won their league with a nine and one record.

The team stopped for supper at the last rest area before their exit. They were leaving the snack bar when the charter bus carrying the Cyclones fans arrived. Laurie loved being cheered by a busload of people wearing the Compton blue and white.

By the time they reached Albany, a light rain was falling. The bus pulled up next to an awning outside the Capitol Hotel, and the team unloaded their luggage.

Laurie shared a room with Grandma, Maggie, and Li. Grandma took up her knitting and settled down in front of the TV. The girls dropped their bags and left to explore the hotel. They stopped to pick up Howard, but he and Coach Preston were absorbed in a basketball game on the all-sports cable channel.

They found the rest of the team in the game room. Laurie and Li were partners and whipped all comers at Ping-Pong. While waiting their turns to play the duo, the others played arcade games. The fun lasted until nine o'clock, when they were due back in their rooms. Whether from the excitement or the long day, all the girls fell asleep quickly.

Coach Preston gave his players a nine o'clock wake-up call. They were to meet in the hotel dining room at nine-thirty for breakfast. The Cyclones would play the first game of the day at noon, giving them plenty of time to digest their food.

While they ate, Laurie checked out their opponents, who were seated at a table on the other side of the room. To her relief, the Mohawk Marauders didn't look any bigger or stronger than the Cyclones.

She also kept an eye on the door leading into the lobby. She was hoping the Bradley Buccaneers would arrive early enough for Christy to watch the Compton game. But since the Buccaneers were the number one seed, they wouldn't play until six o'clock that night and would probably arrive after the Cyclones played.

"It would be so good to see Christy again," Laurie thought. If they were both on winning teams today, there would be lots to celebrate at dinner tonight. But if the Cyclones lost, they would be going home right after the Bradley game. The big reunion between Christy and Laurie would probably last all of five minutes.

After breakfast, most of the girls headed to the game room. Laurie sat in the lobby to watch for Christy. To keep herself entertained, she read magazines and tried to guess what each person checking out did for a living. When ten-thirty came and it was time to board the bus for the Hudson Arena, there was still no sign of the Bradley team.

At the arena, Laurie scanned the parking lot to see if the Bradley bus was there. She spotted two school buses, but both bore the red and white logo of the Mohawk Marauders.

Laurie got an eerie feeling walking into the Hudson Arena. The Mohawk fans were already there—two busloads worth—and yet the cavernous arena seemed empty. She had never played in such a large building before. It felt weird to see hundreds of rows of empty seats. The girls whispered nervously to one another, afraid their normal voices would echo in such a huge space.

The locker room, too, seemed strange. It smelled of disinfectant, and the lockers were covered in scratches and dents from the hundreds of teams who had used them through the years. By the time the Cyclones went out for their pregame warmups, Laurie thought her teammates looked as skittish and uncomfortable as she felt.

The Compton spectators had arrived. Mr. Riley and the others let out a whoop when Laurie led the team into view. But the huge building swallowed the sound. The parents and students, who had rocked the cozy Compton gym, seemed insignificant in this larger setting.

With the lay-up drill done, the squad gathered in a circle for their signature passing drill. Howard stood behind Laurie, holding the second and third balls, but it was quite a while before she nodded for them. The Cyclones were so tight that the simplest passes were bobbled. Laurie herself got bopped in the head with a pass from Li. She had been scanning the bleachers, hoping to spot Christy, and hadn't been paying attention to her teammates.

Dawn broke the tension when she smiled and said, "Li's owed you that one since our first practice!"

Motivation

Either the Mohawk team had played in a large arena before, or their players had steadier nerves than the girls from Compton.

The Marauders showed a great touch from the outside. Laurie felt as if Mohawk jump shots were raining down from all angles, and the Cyclones trailed 20 to 8 at the end of the first quarter.

Coach Preston hardly seemed worried. "Get good position for rebounds and let them shoot from outside," he advised. "No team can stay that hot for long."

To Laurie's relief, her dad's advice proved right. The Marauders began to miss the same shots they had sunk when their legs had been fresh. Slowly, the Cyclones crept closer to the lead. When Dawn fed Jackie for a last-second lay-up, Compton was within five points at the half.

Laurie was trotting toward the locker room when she was grabbed from behind. She spun around, and there was Christy. After looking for her everywhere, Laurie had gotten so involved in the game that she had forgotten all about her friend.

"Hey, Laurie, you're looking good!" Christy greeted her.

Laurie doubted that she looked good after playing a tough half of basketball, but it felt great to hear Christy say it. She hugged her best friend for all she was worth.

"Can you stay for the second half?" Laurie asked.

"Only if you promise to win," Christy teased. "How are you going to keep our dinner date tonight if you let these upstaters beat you?"

Laurie vowed to be unstoppable in the second half. She had waited for months to see her friend, and nothing was going to come between them now.

"Don't worry, Christy. We're just toying with them. I'll see you after the game."

When she got to the locker room, Li handed her an orange.

"I'd throw it to you, but I'm afraid I might hit you again," she joked.

"Not to worry, Li. I'm wide awake now," Laurie assured her.

Minutes later, Coach Preston came in.

"Psycho press," he called. "And don't hold anything back. No one is in foul trouble, our bench is deep, and we all want to stay overnight in that great hotel again. Let's send those Marauders back to Mohawk where they belong."

The Cyclones whooped with excitement and charged out of the locker room and back onto the court.

Laurie had played some great games for the Cyclones this season. But her teammates had never seen her as inspired as she was at the start of that second half. Her determination to spend the weekend with Christy gave Laurie complete concentration.

During the first half, playing in such a huge arena, Laurie had felt like a flea scurrying around on the back of a Great Dane. Now her focus was so intense that nothing existed off the court. She played as loosely as if she were playing in her driveway back in Bradley.

Time and again, she stole the ball, and the Marauders began to lose their poise along with their lead. The basket looked so big that Laurie felt she couldn't miss. Her shots poured through the hoop until the Marauders could only shake their heads, their shoulders sagging in defeat.

When Coach Preston took Laurie out with two minutes left in the game, the Compton fans, and even some of the Mohawk supporters, gave her a standing ovation. Laurie didn't look at the score until she flopped on the bench, a towel over her shoulders. To her amazement, Compton was fourteen points ahead. Her effort had helped secure a victory for the Cyclones.

The locker room was filled with cheers and laughter, but Laurie went straight to the showers. She couldn't wait to get back in the gym and spend some time with Christy.

It was now around two o'clock, and Laurie knew that by four-thirty, the Bradley coach would call his team together to begin preparing for their six o'clock game.

As they left the locker room, Coach Preston told the girls that they were free to go anywhere in the arena but no one could leave the building without his permission. Li yelled for Laurie to meet her and the rest of the Cyclones at the concession stands. But Laurie made a beeline for Christy.

Chapter 8

High Powered

The second game of the tournament was being played far below, but Christy and Laurie had no idea who was winning. They sat by themselves in the top row of the arena. E-mail, snail mail, or the telephone couldn't equal talking facc to face.

Christy had news about the kids in Bradley, the teachers she and Laurie knew, and the town itself. As Laurie listened, she felt that she had been away from Bradley for years instead of three short months. She, in turn, had loads of things to tell Christy about her new friends and teammates.

When the second half started, hunger drove the best friends to the concession stands. With everyone else's attention on the game, they were free to eat and talk undisturbed. They heard cheers from courtside, but they devoted their full attention to each other. They talked about spring vacation and how to convince their folks to let them spend it together.

Then a Bradley player named Becky ran up to them. "Hi, Laurie!" she called. "How have you been?"

Laurie barely had time to say hi before Becky turned to Christy. "Coach Benson sent me to find you. Team meeting in five minutes in our locker room."

Laurie wished Christy luck in her game and walked back toward the court. Christy gave her a wave and trotted after Becky.

Laurie checked the scoreboard and saw that the third game of the day had started. Since the Cyclones would play the winner of this contest, she decided to see how the teams looked.

The number two seed, the Delano Demons, were off to a quick start. They led the Sterling Silvers by ten points. When the first quarter ended, Laurie looked around until she spotted Howard sitting high up in the stands with his laptop plugged into an outlet. She made the long climb to his perch.

"How do the Demons look, How?" she asked.

"They're going to win easily, Laurie. This Sterling team is weak."

Laurie spent the rest of the game alternating between watching the action on the court and watching Howard pound stats into his laptop. It amazed her that someone who couldn't keep his sneakers tied could type so quickly.

Just as Howard had predicted, the Demons won easily. When the Delano coach cleared his bench with five minutes left to play—and a twenty-four point lead—Howard had all the information he needed.

"Let's grab something to eat before Bradley comes out to warm up," he said.

Laurie and Howard scampered down the long aisle to courtside and walked out to the concession stand. Laurie waited patiently as Howard got himself a couple of hot dogs covered in mustard and relish and got her a personal pizza. At last, she asked the key question.

"Well, do you think we can beat them?"

"I know we can—as long as your dad listens to me. If you let the Demons do what they want, they'll chew up any team. But I spotted a weakness," Howard boasted.

"What is it?" Laurie asked impatiently.

"I need some time to study my data. I'll talk to your dad in our room tonight."

Laurie would have pushed Howard further, but just then they heard the final buzzer, and the Delano Demon fans came storming out to celebrate.

"Christy will be warming up!" Laurie shouted. "Let's go, Howard!"

Domination

For this game, there was no way Laurie was going to sit in the nosebleed seats with Howard. She wanted to be courtside while Christy was playing.

Li had saved Laurie a spot in the front row, but before Laurie could settle into it, she heard voices calling, "Laurie!"

She shrugged her shoulders apologetically to Li and climbed the stairs to the third row. Laurie didn't notice the hurt look on Li's face. She moved along the row saying hi to friends, neighbors, and classmates from Bradley.

In a way it made Laurie feel sad to be reunited with these people. She realized she missed so many familiar faces, not just Christy's. There was Mr. Constantino, who used to give her a cookie whenever she stopped in his bakery. She met Pete, the mailman, who had often shot a basket or two in her driveway before continuing his route. Even Ms. Marston, whom Laurie had never seen outside the Bradley town library before, was at the game.

Laurie squeezed into a space between Nancy and Sheila, two girls who had been her classmates from kindergarten through fourth grade. Between the attention and the delicious anticipation of seeing Christy play, she forgot about Li, who sat alone.

For Bradley fans, the game was fun to watch. For everyone else, it was a bore. Christy and the other Buccaneers were far superior to the Chelsea Wildcats. The Bradley team did what it wanted, when it wanted. The game was never in doubt, and Coach Benson subbed players early and often to keep his team from running up the score. Despite his efforts, Bradley won by nearly forty points.

The moment the game ended, Laurie searched for her dad. She found him in the referees' office, talking with the officials. Coach Preston embarrassed Laurie by introducing her as "my daughter and star player."

Laurie nodded politely, then dragged her father to the door.

"Dad, can I ride back with Christy if Coach Benson says it's okay?" she asked.

"I guess so, Laurie, but don't you want to ride with your teammates? We've got an important game tomorrow."

"Dad, I haven't seen Christy in three months! This might be our one night to spend time together."

Coach Preston smiled. "Come on," he said, "We'll talk to Coach Benson together."

Coach Benson told them that the Buccaneers weren't heading back to the hotel but to a sports legends restaurant for a celebration dinner. He said Laurie was welcome to join them. Coach Preston made sure Laurie had money, kissed her good-bye, and left to round up his team.

Laurie entered the happy Bradley locker room. She hugged her friends and joined the fun. On the bus, she sang the Bradley school songs and shouted the familiar cheers. Once she slipped and started singing "We Are the Champions." When the other girls fell silent, she realized her mistake. It was the only time she felt out of place.

She and Christy loved the restaurant. There was a whole room devoted to basketball. Christy took a picture of Laurie standing next to a life-size statue of her namesake, Larry Bird.

By the time they got back to the Capitol Hotel, Laurie was exhausted. When she entered her room, she woke Grandma, who had been dozing in front of the TV.

"The others are in the game room, Laurie. Just call your dad to tell him you're back before you go down," she said.

"Thanks, Grandma, but I thought I might stay in Christy's room. The hotel can set up a cot, and we can watch the late movie together. Our game's not until four tomorrow, so I don't have to get up early."

"It's up to your father, Laurie. But don't neglect your teammates. Li has called twice looking for you. I told her I was sure you'd visit the game room when you got in."

"Grandma, I can see Li anytime. If one of us loses tomorrow, Christy and I will be apart again. I want to spend time with her while I can."

"Why not take Christy to the game room?" Grandma suggested. "That way you can spend time with her and your teammates."

"It's not the same. Christy and I want to talk. We don't want anyone else hanging around."

Grandma didn't look convinced of Laurie's reasoning. And Coach Preston didn't seem pleased with Laurie's plan either when she called him. But he knew how much she had missed Christy, so he gave in.

Isolation

Laurie was dreaming that she and Christy were being introduced to a screaming crowd at Madison Square Garden when a ringing telephone jarred her awake. The best friends had stayed up long after the other girls had fallen asleep, whispering and giggling while watching old movies on TV.

Christy staggered to the phone.

"It's your dad, Laurie," she said, flopping back into bed.

Laurie inched herself off the cot and across the room.

"Dad, what time is it?" she mumbled.

"It's ten-thirty, sleepyhead. Get dressed. The team meets in the dining room at eleven."

"Can Christy come, too?"

"Not this time, Laurie. We need to talk about our game today. I'm sure Coach Benson will be looking for Christy before long anyway."

Laurie wanted to wish Christy luck, but her friend had fallen back to sleep. She scribbled a note on a pad she found next to the phone and left it sticking out of one of Christy's sneakers.

When her teammates barely said hello, Laurie thought they

were as sleepy as she was. It didn't occur to her that the Cyclones might feel that she had abandoned them to hang out with an opponent.

Li had usually saved Laurie a seat, but this time the chairs on both sides of her were taken. So Laurie sat next to Howard, who had his laptop open on the table.

"What did my dad think of your scouting report on the Demons?" Laurie asked.

"He won't even look at it," Howard complained. "He's got some big plan of his own that he's going to unveil."

"Do you know what it is?"

"Are you kidding? Your father only thinks of me when someone needs water or a towel," Howard said disgustedly. "It's no fun spending two nights in a room with a guy who won't really talk with you."

Laurie was trying to think of something to say to make Howard feel better when her father stood to start the meeting.

"Girls, the hotel is going to serve us an early lunch as soon as we're done here. Then you're free until two o'clock when the bus leaves for the arena. Remember not to leave the hotel without permission."

Coach Preston waited until the players finished whispering their plans to one another. Then he went on.

"Most of you saw our opponents, the Delano Demons, play. They are a fine team. We're a fine team as well. But it's going to take our best game to beat them."

Coach Preston looked around the table to make sure all the girls were as serious as he was.

"We're going to try something different. As soon as we score our first basket, throw on the Psycho Press. Maybe we can take them by surprise and get an early lead."

He waited again as the girls buzzed with excitement. Li and the other substitutes loved it when the Cyclones pressed. It meant that everyone got to play a lot of minutes.

"Whatever happens today, you can all be proud of this season. Win or lose, we'll stay to see the second game between Bradley and Tremont. If we lose, we'll vote on whether to stay for the championship game tomorrow or go home tonight."

He waved to a server standing in the doorway. Within minutes the girls were eating fruit cups. They ordered sandwiches from the menu and had ice cream for dessert.

Laurie tried to draw Howard into a conversation, but he was brooding, pecking at the keys on his laptop. He wouldn't say anything about the Cyclones' chances, but his attitude told Laurie a lot. Howard thought they were going to lose—and lose badly.

After lunch, Laurie followed the others to the game room. She hoped to be Li's partner in Ping-Pong, but Li chose to play with Angela.

"Where's the Bradley Bomber?" Li asked her. "Maybe you could be partners with her."

Laurie felt her face redden. The other girls stopped playing their games to see what would happen next. Couldn't Li understand anything? It wasn't that Laurie didn't like Li. It was just that she had waited so long to see Christy. Was it wrong to want to spend time with your best friend?

Laurie turned and walked out of the game room. She was

halfway down the hall when she heard the Ping-Pong and arcade games start up again.

Pressure

Laurie made sure she was in the lobby at five minutes before two. She wasn't about to be late for the bus and give her teammates another reason to be mad at her.

The two hours of free time had passed slowly with no friends to help while them away. Laurie had gone back to her room and watched soaps with Grandma. Since she didn't care about the programs, the background noise mixed with the clicking of Grandma's needles had helped her think. She'd decided that the quickest way to win back her teammates' affections would be to play her hardest today. Surely, if she led them to the championship game, the girls couldn't stay mad at her.

By the time the game was five minutes old, she and the Cyclones were united again. But not in the way Laurie had hoped. The players were united in misery over a terrible start.

The famed Psycho Press, which had brought them so much success, was a disaster against Delano. The well-coached Demons broke the press with ease. They seldom dribbled and instead whipped passes over and around the scrambling Cyclones. Jesse picked up two quick fouls, and the Demons scored at will.

Then Li landed on the foot of a rebounding Delano player and fell to the floor, gripping her ankle. Mrs. Tang was on the court nearly as quickly as Coach Preston. She and her husband helped Li to the locker room while Howard went to the trainer's room for ice packs.

When Coach Preston called a time-out, Laurie was relieved to see that the Cyclones were only fourteen points behind. The beating had felt much worse.

Coach Preston took off the press. The Cyclones played the Demons evenly for the rest of the first half. But no matter what defense they played, they couldn't seem to cut Delano's lead. When the teams headed for their locker rooms at the half, the score was Delano 36, Compton 24.

Laurie trudged across the arena, a towel around her neck. Her teammates might not be mad at her anymore, but they looked as down as she felt. She hoped that Li was all right. She wondered if her father had any ideas to help them cut the Delano lead.

Howard came running up just as Laurie reached the locker room door. He stuck his laptop in her face.

"You've got to get your father to look at these shooting charts. He just told me to get lost," Howard complained.

Laurie stared at the screen. The display showed the outline of a basketball court from the top of the key to the basket. Different spots on the court were dotted with tiny sets of numbers. On the right side, Laurie saw number combinations like 8/10, 7/11, and 6/9. The combinations on the left read 1/8, 0/6, 2/12, and so on.

"What does this mean, Howard?" she asked impatiently

"Those are shooting records for the first game Delano played plus the first half of this game. The front number in each pair shows how many shots they made from that spot on the floor. The second number is shots taken."

Laurie whistled softly. "According to this, they're nearly

helpless from the left side!"

"I tried to tell your father last night. If you guys overplay everything on the right and leave the left side open, you can shut this team down!" Howard shouted.

At that moment, Coach Preston came toward the locker room. He was nervously running his fingers through his hair.

"Laurie, tell the girls I'm coming in, please," he said flatly.

"First look at this, Dad," Laurie answered, extending the laptop toward her father.

Coach Preston waved off the suggestion.

"Laurie, I was coaching before there were computers. I don't need to look at stats to know we're getting whipped."

"Dad, Howard's got a plan. Please just give him one minute. You can't have that much to say in there," Laurie said, pointing toward the locker room.

Reluctantly, Coach Preston took the laptop. Howard jumped into his explanation. Within a minute, Coach Preston was looking over his shoulder to make sure no one from Delano had overheard. After Laurie warned the girls that he was coming in, Coach Preston grabbed Howard's elbow and steered him into the locker room.

Five minutes later, he had explained the new game plan to the Cyclones.

"Coach, no offense, but are you sure Howard knows what he's talking about?" Dawn looked at Howard with her eyebrows raised.

"Stats don't lie!" Howard spat.

Coach Preston looked away from his doubting players and into Howard's eyes. Howard stared back fiercely, ready to back his claims against anyone's.

Coach Preston sighed, "Ladies, this may be our one chance to win. None of our normal defenses has stopped them. Let's try this and see if it works."

When the Delano Demons scored the first two baskets of the second half on a lay-up and a jumper from the left side, Howard sunk down in his seat at Coach Preston's side.

Then the Demons started to miss. Dawn and Laurie overplayed the Delano guards to such an extreme that they couldn't resist dribbling or passing to a wide-open left side.

The suddenly hopeful Cyclones swept the boards and fired passes to Dawn and Laurie, who began breaking for the hoop in anticipation of missed shots.

The score grew closer. Li squirmed on the bench, her ankle wrapped in ice, frustrated at not being able to play. Mr. and Mrs. Tang had wanted Li to go to the emergency room and have her ankle examined. But Li refused to leave until the game was over. Her cheers made Laurie feel forgiven and part of the team again.

The Demons began to show their nerves, making useless fouls on Compton fast breaks that they had no hope of stopping. Dawn and Laurie looked as if they could shoot free throws all night without missing.

When Laurie finished a three-point play with thirteen seconds left, the Cyclones led for the first time 62 to 61. If they could stop Delano one more time, the game would be theirs.

Laurie overplayed the dribble as the Demons' point guard came to the top of the key. When her opponent passed the ball to the left side, Laurie came out of her crouch and peeked at the clock. In that split second, the player she was guarding cut to the hoop.

Laurie recovered quickly, but the return pass eluded her fingertips. She watched helplessly as the Demon point guard—who was her responsibility—drove in uncontested toward the hoop.

The Demon player went up to bank her shot off the glass. At the same instant, Maggie leaped straight into the air. Laurie was sure Maggie was too far away to affect the shot, but Maggie's hand kept rising.

Just before the ball reached its apex, Maggie brushed it with her fingertips. The shot hit the backboard an inch too low and spun off the rim. Jackie grabbed the rebound as the buzzer sounded, and Laurie fell to her knees in relief.

The Cyclones were going to the championship game!

Injured Reserve

Only a Delano fan could have walked past the door of the Cyclones' locker room without smiling. When Laurie opened the locker room door and helped Li walk out to her waiting parents, the two girls found Howard sitting with his back against the wall, hugging his laptop and listening to the wild celebration inside.

He told them he should be in the stands to chart the Bradley game, but he couldn't tear himself away from his team. For the first time, he felt like a full member of the Cyclones. Coach Preston had followed his advice, and it had paid off.

When the locker room suddenly became silent, Howard looked questioningly at Laurie and Li, but they just grinned at him. He slid over and leaned his head against the door, trying to hear what was going on inside.

Suddenly the door flew open. Before Howard could fall, eight pairs of hands grabbed him. The players stood Howard up, mussed his hair, clapped him on the back, and hugged him, all the while chanting his name.

Howard struggled to free himself, but he looked as if he loved every bit of the attention. At last, the Cyclones released him. He asked Laurie if she was ready to go watch Christy. To his surprise, Laurie shook her head, ducked back into the locker room, and came out wearing her coat.

"Tell my dad I'll be at the emergency room with Li," Laurie called. "I'll see you back at the hotel."

Li's face lit up when Laurie asked the Tangs if she could go to the emergency room with them. During the taxi ride, the girls talked excitedly about the tournament.

"I'll be ready tomorrow," Li said. "No ankle is going to make me miss the championship game."

Mr. and Mrs. Tang didn't say anything. They looked as if they doubted that Li would be able to play but didn't want to be the ones to tell her.

Ninety minutes later, Laurie sat next to Li in the waiting room at Albany General Hospital. The room was noisy, hot, and crowded. The two girls leaned against each other and dozed. It had been a long, exciting weekend, but neither girl would know until they returned to the hotel that the most important part was still to come. Christy had led the Buccaneers to an easy victory over the Tremont Tempests. Bradley would play Compton at noon on Presidents' Day for the New York State Middle School Championship.

The Finals

Lining up for the opening tap, Laurie felt every nerve in her body tingle. The huge arena was far from full, but the biggest crowd of the tournament was on hand. Even the teams eliminated in yesterday's action, as well as many of their fans, showed up to see the championship game.

The noise coming from the stands almost overwhelmed Laurie. Both the Buccaneer and Cyclone fans seemed to think whoever cheered the loudest would decide which team would win. She thought back to the days when Howard had done everything but beg the fans to cheer, only to be met with silence. How things had changed!

Howard now sat in his new seat of honor next to Coach Preston. Li sat next to Howard. Her ankle was tightly taped, but she was dressed in full uniform. The x-rays had proven no bones were broken, and her parents had agreed that she could play.

Laurie looked across the circle and met Christy's gaze. The best friends smiled and gave each other a thumbs-up for good luck. The referee stepped in between Maggie and the Bradley center, and Laurie quickly focused on the game.

Maggie tipped the ball to Jackie, who passed it to Dawn. Dawn found Laurie, and the Cyclones set up their offense. After working the ball around, Laurie got it to Jesse, who shot from behind Maggie's screen. The shot was on target, and the Cyclones had the lead.

Both offenses worked deliberately; neither defense was giving up fast breaks or cheap baskets. At the half, the Cyclones led by a single point, with the score 24 to 23.

As she jogged into the locker room, Laurie hoped her father wouldn't call for the Psycho Press. She thought that Christy and her teammates would handle it just as efficiently as the Delano Demons had. She was afraid that if the Cyclones fell behind, the excellent Bradley defense might make it impossible for Compton to catch up.

Li was bouncing off the locker room walls, determined to show she was ready to play. Dawn had held Christy to eight points, but she had picked up three fouls in the process. Coach Preston reluctantly named Li to start the second half in Dawn's spot.

For the first few minutes, the strategy seemed to work. Twice the Buccaneers brought the ball up, and twice Li forced Christy to pass. Then Christy drove toward the hoop, forcing Li to cut sharply to keep up. Li stumbled, and as she clutched her ankle, the Cyclones knew her season was over.

Laurie helped Li to their bench.

"Great job, Li," Laurie said, hugging her. "You were really shutting Christy down."

Li grimaced either from pain or from disappointment. But then she smiled and whispered, "You can do it, Laurie." Laurie smiled back.

Dawn again guarded Christy, but Christy took advantage of Dawn's foul trouble. She drove toward the hoop each time she got the ball, and Dawn had little choice but to let her pass by untouched. Jesse and Maggie made quick adjustments under the basket, but more often than not, the Buccaneers scored.

Slowly but surely, Bradley began to pull away. When the

buzzer announced the end of the third quarter, the Buccaneers had a six-point lead.

"Ladies, this is it," Coach Preston began when the Cyclones reached their bench. "Dawn, don't hold back any longer. Play your tightest defense. If you pick up a fourth foul, you and Laurie can switch players. Their point guard would much rather pass than shoot."

Laurie's heart pounded. She didn't want to guard Christy. What if she stopped Christy and made her best friend look bad? Christy might never forgive her.

Then Laurie thought of a worse outcome. Suppose she couldn't stop Christy. Would the other Cyclones think she had played her soft because she and Christy were friends? Her teammates had thought she was disloyal just for spending time with Christy on Saturday night.

The buzzer sounded, and there was no more time to think. Laurie took Dawn's inbound pass and led the team up court. She threw the ball to Maggie at the foul line, and Maggie kicked it out to Jackie. Jackie's shot split the cords, and the Cyclones were within four points.

When she got the ball, Christy tried to force Dawn to foul her. And when Dawn beat Christy to a spot, the two girls collided. The referee blew his whistle, and all eyes darted to him. He slapped his hand behind his head, signaling an offensive foul. The Cyclones had the ball.

Laurie hit a jumper to get the Cyclones within two points. Then the teams traded baskets until a minute remained. Christy missed a shot from just outside the foul line. Dawn vied for the rebound, and the referee's whistle blew. After avoiding her fourth foul while guarding Christy, Dawn had just been called for reaching over her back on a rebound.

Dawn hung her head, then snapped it up. She grabbed Laurie's elbow and whispered in her ear, "It's up to you, Laurie."

Laurie didn't need the reminder. The lump in her throat told her that it was her responsibility to stop Christy now.

The Bradley point guard inbounded, and Christy dribbled toward the top of the key. Laurie grudgingly gave Christy ground. She stayed in her crouch, her eyes focused on Christy's waist. She knew that a player might fake with her hands, feet, or eyes, but not with her waist. If Christy committed to shooting or driving, the movement of her waist would warn Laurie.

Christy faked right, faked left, and then went up for her silky jump shot. Laurie couldn't block the shot, but she was close enough to put a hand in Christy's face. The pressure was just enough to make Christy miss the shot, and Jesse grabbed the rebound.

Jesse whipped a pass to Laurie. Laurie dribbled up court, watching Dawn from the corner of her eye. When Laurie forced the ball down the lane, Dawn's defender came over to shut her off. Laurie bounced a pass to Dawn, whose open jumper rattled the rim before dropping in for two points. With twenty seconds left, the score was tied.

Coach Benson called for a time-out, and the jubilant Cyclones swept Dawn toward their bench. Coach Preston warned the girls that Compton had used all their time-outs. If Bradley scored, the Cyclones had to get the ball up court and make a basket before time expired.

Laurie thought she might throw up. She knew Christy would come after her again, and she didn't know if she could stop her. She would love to keep Christy from getting the ball, but she was afraid that if she played in front of her, Christy might sneak away and be wide open.

When play resumed, Laurie hounded Christy as they trotted up the floor. Christy easily caught a pass thrown above Laurie's reach, then whipped the ball back to her point guard. Christy cut for the hoop, but Laurie knew what her friend was up to. She had seen Christy run this play a thousand times. She let Christy go and darted into the passing lane.

The ball came and Laurie snatched it. She dribbled behind her back and raced around the Bradley point guard. In full flight now, she streaked toward the basket at the far end of the gym. She heard the fans screaming the countdown as she reached the foul line. Five! Four! Three!

One final defender waited in a crouch, her eyes glued to Laurie's. Laurie's head bobbed as if she were pulling up for a jumper. The defender's feet left the floor, and Laurie zipped around her.

Laurie's heart raced. All she had to do was sink a lay-up, and the game would be over. At that instant, her left foot slipped on a wet spot left moments before by two sweating players vying for a loose ball. The crowd gasped.

As she plummeted toward the floor, Laurie flipped the ball toward the basket. She heard the buzzer as the ball teetered on the rim. Laurie begged it to drop. After what seemed like an eternity, it fell softly through the net.

Tears welled in Laurie's eyes as her teammates stampeded toward the leader of their championship team.

Awards

The sign on the door of the Slice of Life read "Closed for Private Party." It was Friday night, and Ralph had turned his place over to the Cyclones and their families for a victory celebration.

Laurie had smiled so much this past week that her face hurt. She couldn't walk anywhere in the school—or in town, for that matter—without receiving congratulations for winning the championship.

Only one thing had bothered her, though. She and Christy had exchanged hugs after the game but hadn't spoken since then. Laurie had sent her an e-mail as soon as she got back from Albany, but Christy hadn't responded. Could her best friend be mad at her because she had beaten her in the big game?

Laurie sat near Li, whose ankle rested on a chair between them. Yesterday Li had reported that her ankle was completely healed, yet tonight she insisted that she needed to elevate it. She wouldn't let anyone sit between herself and Laurie.

Their friendship was better than ever. Because Laurie had gone to the emergency room with her instead of staying at the arena to watch Christy play, Li knew that she was important to Laurie, too.

Just then Mr. Tang came in. He carried an overnight bag.

Li whispered, "Laurie, my father and I wanted to do something nice for you, since you were such a good friend to me in Albany."

Christy stepped out from behind Mr. Tang. She ran across the room, hugged Laurie, then dropped into the empty chair.

"Mr. Tang drove up and got me," she explained. "I can stay all weekend. Sunday morning, you and your dad are taking me back."

Laurie's eyes filled with tears. "I thought you were mad at me because we won the game. I didn't want to guard you, but I had to do my best."

Christy smiled. "Do you think I would have wanted to win because you didn't play your hardest? The better team won. But I would like to guard you again someday—and for more than two plays!"

"Maybe next year we'll make it to the tourney again," Laurie said. "Let's go to the mall and catch a movie tomorrow."

"I'm there," Christy answered.

Laurie turned to Li. "Can you go to the movies with us?" she asked.

"Sure," Li beamed.

A glistening three-foot-high silver trophy sat in the center of the team table. A figurine of a girl releasing a jump shot topped it. A plaque mounted on the base bore the inscription *Compton Cyclones*, and underneath were the words *New York State Middle School Champions: Small-School Division*.

When his guests had eaten and drunk their fill, Ralph flicked the light switch up and down to signal for quiet. He asked everyone to raise their sodas high in honor of his friend and teammate, Coach Preston.

"He was a winner when we were young, he's a winner today, and he's passed his game and his attitude to his daughter, Laurie, and the rest of the Cyclones."

Laurie's face reddened as everyone cheered. Coach Preston got up to speak. He carried a package wrapped in bright paper under one arm.

"Some teams have award dinners at the end of the season," he began. "Well, our award is sitting in the middle of this table. That trophy shows what can happen when a group puts aside its differences and learns to play together as a team."

A round of cheering stopped Coach Preston for a moment. Then he went on.

"I'm not going to give a Most Valuable Player award. Each and every member of the team did something special to help us pull out a victory. If any one of those wins had been losses, we never would have been invited to the state tournament. So it's a ten-way tie for MVP."

Again the cheers of parents and players forced Coach Preston to stop.

"But there is one person whose contribution I overlooked, almost until it was too late. This special award goes to Howard Goldstein. Without his computerized scouting report, I don't think we could have beaten Delano."

Howard's jaw dropped. He walked to Coach Preston's side of the table and faced the crowd, his shirt dotted with pizza stains.

Coach Preston handed him the package. Howard set it on the table, spilling a couple of sodas in the process. He tore off the wrapping paper, reached into the box and pulled out—a laptop battery.

"Howard, with that new battery, your laptop should stay charged up for an entire game. From now on, I want you and your stats near me at games, not up on top of the bleachers where you have to plug in."

Howard was speechless, but his grin showed his gratitude.

The next surprise was from Grandma. When her son asked her to stand, Ralph and two of his employees brought in what looked like a rolled-up blanket from one of the backrooms. They held it in front of them while Grandma spoke.

"This has been the most exciting year. I'm so pleased to have my son and my granddaughter living with me. And I'm happy that you other girls let me be part of your lives, too."

"You know I'm always knitting, but did you realize you've never seen a finished product? Maggie helped me connect all the separate pieces I knitted. Here's what I have to show for a long and happy season."

When Grandma nodded, Ralph and the others unrolled the "blanket" to reveal a huge knitted banner. It read "Compton Cyclones" in the bright-blue and white team colors.

When the crowd's cheering finally faded, Coach Preston promised the banner would hang in the gym for as long as he was the coach.

"Now, I have one last duty to perform for this season," he said with great seriousness. Then his face broke into a smile. "We are the champions, my friends!" he crooned.

Laurie wrapped one arm around Christy, the other around Li, and sang for all she was worth.

Also from Meadowbrook Press

✦ ***Troop 13: The Mystery of the Haunted Caves***
Four girls participating in the Gold Rush Jamboree with their scout troop happen upon a mysterious map hinting at treasure buried in the Haunted Caves. Becca and her three friends are determined to find the treasure, even if it means sneaking from camp, exploring bat-filled caves, and risking their safety when robbers threaten them...

✦ ***Girls to the Rescue series***
Girls save the day in this critically acclaimed anthology series, where clever, courageous, and determined girls from around the world rise to the occassion in hair-raising tales of adventure, and...come to the rescue.

✦ ***Free Stuff for Kids***
The number one kids' activity book! Published yearly, with hundreds of free and up-to-a-dollar offers children can send for through the mail, including stickers, crafts, hobbies, and Internet offers.

✦ ***What Do You Know About Manners?***
A book about manners that kids will enjoy reading? Absolutely, and parents will love it, too. It's filled with fun, imaginative ways to fine-tune a child's manners, and presented in a humurous format with over 100 quiz items and illustrations.

We offer many more titles written to delight, inform, and entertain.

To order books with a credit card, or browse our full selection of titles, visit our website at:

www.meadowbrookpress.com

or call toll-free to place an order, request a free catalog, or ask a question:

1-800-338-2232

Meadowbrook Press • 5451 Smetana Drive • Minnetonka, MN • 55343